PUFFIN BOOKS

GRANDMA'S BAG OF STORIES

Sudha Murty was born in 1950 in Shiggaon in north Karnataka. She did her M.Tech in computer science, and is now the chairperson of the Infosys Foundation. A prolific writer in English and Kannada, she has written novels, technical books, travelogues, collections of short stories and non-fiction pieces and three books for children, *How I Taught My Grandmother to Read and Other Stories*, *The Magic Drum and Other Favourite Stories* and *The Bird with Golden Wings: Stories of Wit and Magic* all available in Puffin.

Her books have been translated into all the major Indian languages and have sold over four lakh copies around the country. She was the recipient of the R.K. Narayan's Award for Literature and the Padma Shri in 2006, and the Attimabbe Award from the Government of Karnataka for excellence in Kannada literature in 2011.

GRANDMA'S BAG OF STORIES

SUDHA MURTY

Illustrations by
Priya Kuriyan

PUFFIN BOOKS

PUFFIN BOOKS

Published by the Penguin Group

Penguin Books India Pvt. Ltd, 11 Community Centre, Panchsheel Park, New Delhi 110 017, India

Penguin Group (USA) Inc., 375 Hudson Street, New York, New York 10014, USA

Penguin Group (Canada), 90 Eglinton Avenue East, Suite 700, Toronto, Ontario, M4P 2Y3, Canada (a division of Pearson Penguin Canada Inc.)

Penguin Books Ltd, 80 Strand, London WC2R 0RL, England

Penguin Ireland, 25 St Stephen's Green, Dublin 2, Ireland (a division of Penguin Books Ltd)

Penguin Group (Australia), 707 Collins Street, Melbourne, Victoria 3008, Australia (a division of Pearson Australia Group Pty Ltd)

Penguin Group (NZ), 67 Apollo Drive, Rosedale, Auckland 0632, New Zealand (a division of Pearson New Zealand Ltd)

Penguin Group (South Africa) (Pty) Ltd, Block D, Rosebank Office Park, 181 Jan Smuts Avenue, Parktown North, Johannesburg 2193, South Africa

Penguin Books Ltd, Registered Offices: 80 Strand, London WC2R 0RL, England

First published in Puffin by Penguin Books India 2012

Copyright © Sudha Murty 2012

Illustration copyright © Priya Kuriyan 2012

All rights reserved

12 11 10 9 8 7 6

ISBN 9780143332022

Typeset in sabon by InoSoft Systems, Noida
Printed at Manipal Technologies Ltd, Manipal

ALWAYS LEARNING   **PEARSON**

To Krishnaa, who has taken me back to my childhood memories, from Sudha Ajji

Author's Note

My grandmother, Krishnaa, popularly known as Krishtakka, was very bright and affectionate. She was also a great storyteller. She never gave us any sermons but taught the values of life through her stories. Those stories and values remain with me even now. I spent my childhood carefree, stress-free, with my cousins and grandparents at my hometown Shiggaon, a sleepy town in North Karnataka. We shared everything there, whatever we had, and that became a great bond among us cousins. The binding force was my grandmother.

I made some changes when I wrote the stories in this book but mostly it is a true reflection of my childhood.

When my granddaughter Krishnaa was born, she elevated me to the position of grandmother. I realized more than ever the importance of stories, and how much they help children to learn. Hence this book.

I hope, with these stories, children and parents will understand the unique relationship between three generations and will continue to create bonds of love with one another and the older generations in their families.

I would like to thank Penguin Books India, who are always eager to publish my work. I would also like to thank Sudeshna Shome Ghosh, who became a good friend apart from being my editor, in my journey of writing, in the last decade.

Sudha Murty
Bangalore

Contents

The Beginning of the Stories

Summer holidays! Ajji smiled to herself as she waited for two more of her grandchildren to arrive. Raghu and Meenu would be here soon. Anand and Krishna had already arrived with their mother the previous evening. They had been waiting restlessly for their cousins to arrive ever since. Even though Ajji told them Raghu and Meenu would be here the next morning, these two kids just would not listen. They went to the railway station with their grandfather, Ajja, to receive them. The train must have pulled into the tiny railway station of Shiggaon by now, and their grandfather would have hired a taxi to bring them home along with their mother and their stacks of luggage.

Ajji hurried through her bath. She had finished cooking their favourite dishes, and was now wearing a nice, soft cotton sari before going to the veranda to wait for them.

There! There they came! What a noise the children were making! They all nearly tumbled out of the car and came leaping and shouting to her, each wanting to be the first to be hugged by her. Each one wanted to be closest to Ajji.

Soon the children settled down. A visit to Ajji and Ajja's house meant first inspecting the garden to see how much the plants had grown since they last came. Then they went to check on the cows, calves, dog, pups, cats and kittens. Then they all ate huge quantities of Ajji's delicious food. Finally, while their mothers went off to chat and rest, the children gathered around their grandmother for the best part of the holidays—listening to her wonderful stories, particularly in the late afternoon.

Let us too gather under the fast revolving fan, on a mat on the floor, fighting to be nearest to her, and listen in.

'Doctor, Doctor'

The first day, the children asked, 'Ajji, how do you know so many stories?'

Ajji smiled and answered, 'My grandmother told me many stories. Some I read in books. A few I learnt from youngsters like you and the rest from your Ajja.' Then Ajji paused and said, 'I see all of you have grown a lot since the last time I saw you. So before I start telling any stories, I want to know what each of you want to be when you grow up.'

Raghu, who was eleven years old, and the oldest of all, said immediately, 'I want to be an environment scientist.' Meenu who was nine said, 'I have not decided, maybe a computer person like my dad.' Anand, who was ten, said, 'I want to be an astronaut,' and his twin sister Krishna firmly said,

'I want to become a fashion designer.' Ajji smiled. 'I am glad all of you have thought about this. We should always have some aim in life which we must try to achieve while being of help to others. Now let me tell you a story of a person who learnt just such a lesson.'

Shall we too join Ajji and her gang of young friends and hear the story?

⌒

On a blazing hot summer afternoon, an old man came walking down a narrow village path. He was tired and thirsty. Right by the road, he spotted a tiny grocery store. It had a tin roof and mud walls. The shopkeeper sat inside fanning himself and shooing away the flies that were buzzing around in the stifling heat. There was a little bench in front of the store where the villagers met when evening came and the land had cooled down. The old man flopped down on the bench. He was so tired that for a while he could not speak. Finally, he opened his mouth and uttered one word, 'Water!'

Now, this village had been facing a horrible problem for a long time. It was near a great desert and the rains came only once a year to fill its ponds and wells. But the rains had disappeared for the last two years, and the villagers had been making do with water from a faraway stream. Every morning

groups of men and women walked a long distance, filled their pots from the little stream and used that the whole day. Naturally, no one wanted to waste even a drop of this precious water.

Yet how do you say no to a thirsty, tired old man when he asks for water? Without a second thought, the shopkeeper, Ravi, who was very kindhearted, poured out a tumbler of water from his pot and gave it to the old man. The man drank it up greedily. Then he said one more word: 'More!' And without waiting for Ravi to give it to him, he lunged for the pot, picked it up and lifting it to his lips drank up Ravi's entire day's supply of water!

Poor Ravi, what could he do? He just stared in dismay. Then he told himself, 'Never mind. After all, I did help someone in need.'

The stranger, meanwhile, now seemed to feel better. He handed the pot back to Ravi, gave a smile that filled Ravi's heart with warmth and said, 'My son, always be kind like this. Help everyone who comes to you like you helped me, and you will be blessed.' Then he picked up his stick and slowly hobbled down the road. Ravi watched the strange old man disappear into the distance, then returned to his shop.

The afternoon heat grew worse. After a while Ravi felt his head was about to burst with a headache. His lips were parched and his throat hurt, it was so dry. He really needed a drink of water. But the visitor had finished it all up! Hoping to coax a drop or two out of the pot, Ravi lifted it to his lips and tilted it. Imagine his surprise when a gush of water ran down his face! It was sweet, refreshing water which not only quenched his thirst, but wiped out his headache too.

Ravi was staring at the water pot, trying to figure out what had just happened, when Karim limped into his shop. Karim was a young man who had hurt his leg in an accident many years ago which had left him with a limp. When he was unwell or tired, his limp became worse. Karim too flopped down on the bench in front of the store and caught his breath, like the old man. Then he fished out a shopping list from his pocket and handed it to Ravi. As Ravi started packing up the items listed on the paper, Karim opened a little bundle of food and ate his lunch sitting on the bench. Finally he wiped his mouth on his scarf and pointed to Ravi's pot of water. 'Mind if I take a little sip? It is so hot after all.'

Ravi was busy measuring out some dal. He said without looking up, 'I would be happy to offer you some, but someone's already had most of it. Then I was feeling unwell and I think I finished the last of it.'

'What are you saying, my friend? I can clearly see the pot brimming over with water!'

Ravi looked up and stared in disbelief. In front of his eyes, Karim poured out a tumblerful of water and drank it. Then he paid for all his groceries and left the store.

Did his limp look as if it was nearly gone? Ravi watched him for a while trying to figure out, then decided the heat was playing tricks on his mind and went back into the cool comfort of his shop and dozed off.

He woke with a start as someone was calling his name urgently. He opened his eyes to find Karim back. This time he was holding by the hand his little sister Fatima. 'Brother wake up, we need your help,' Karim urged.

'Wh-what? Is something wrong?'

'Fatima is burning up with fever!'

'Then go to a doctor, why have you got her to a grocery shop?'

Karim stared at him and said, 'You mean you don't know how you just helped me? My leg, which has been troubling me for the last many years healed up on its own, as soon as I drank the water from your magic pitcher! Give Fatima a drink from it too, I am sure her fever will disappear in no time.'

Ravi was astounded. Magic pitcher? Healing water? What *was* Karim going on about? Nonetheless he passed the pot to Fatima. She drank a bit, then sat down to rest. Within minutes she lifted her head and said, 'It is true, brothers! I am indeed cured of the fever!'

Soon the news spread in the village like wildfire. Ravi, the quiet, kind grocery storekeeper, was now the owner of a magic pitcher, the waters from which could heal anyone of any disease. Every night Ravi left the pitcher in the store, and in the morning it would be filled to the brim with sweet, cool water. Daily, a queue of sick people and their relatives collected in front of his shop. To each one Ravi gave a drink of the water, and they went away saying they were now better. The pot was never empty. Ravi realized the old man he had helped must have given him this gift in gratitude. Ravi understood what a great gift it was and thanked him daily in his mind.

Soon his little store turned into a hospital! Ravi did not charge a paisa for the water. People would leave some money, some gifts for him, and others did not pay him anything but he was still happy with that.

One day, a rich landlord's servant appeared at his doorstep and said, 'My master is unwell. Come with me and give him a drink of your water.'

Ravi replied, 'See the crowd of people behind you, waiting for their turn. How can I leave without helping them and go to your master? Do you think these sick people can stand in the sun for long? Tell your master to come to me instead and I will give him the water here.'

The servant said, 'Ravi, what will you get by helping these poor people? A few rupees? Some rice and dal? Come to my master's house. He will shower you with money and gifts. Your worries about making ends meet will be over for at least a month.'

Ravi was tempted. It was true, why not cure one rich man and get some help in buying his daily needs? Ravi told the people waiting outside to come back the next day and went with the servant to the landlord.

Slowly, in this way, Ravi changed. Where once he could not bear to see the pain and sadness of the sick and poor people, he now started each day hoping he would get one rich patient at least, who would pay him handsomely.

Days passed thus. Seasons changed and it was summer once more. Ravi was in his old store, writing up his accounts, when the voice of an old man quavered in his ear, 'Son, water!'

Startled, he looked up. Was it the same old man who had given him the gift of the magic pitcher? But right behind the visitor was none other than the king's messenger. 'Come quickly!' the messenger shouted. 'The queen has been bitten by a mosquito!'

'Water!' the old man repeated.

'The queen is unwell!' the messenger shouted again.

Ravi looked from one to the other. One was a grubby old man who may or may not be the same person who gave him the pitcher. On the other side a messenger from the king himself! He pictured the gold coins showering down on him once his healing water soothed the queen's mosquito bites. The choice was clear.

He picked up his pitcher and said to the stranger, 'Wait right here, Uncle, I'll be back soon.'

The king's swift-footed horses took him to the palace. There he rushed to the queen who was staring in dismay at the mosquito-bites on her arm. He tilted the pitcher to pour some water into a tumbler, but nothing came! Again and again he tilted the pitcher. He turned it upside down and stared into its depths. It was dry as bone.

'You cheat!' the king roared. 'So this is how you have been fooling the people of my kingdom! Get out, and never let me hear that you have acquired magical healing powers. If you claim such a thing again I will banish you forever from the village.' Then he turned to comfort his queen who was splashing tears on the bump on her arm.

Ravi slowly walked back to his village. He went to his shop. No one was there. He searched for the old man who had asked for water. He was nowhere to be seen. He called out, 'Uncle, I am sorry. I made a mistake. Please do come. I will give you water.' But there was no reply. Now he realized this was the same old man whom he met a year back.

He remembered the people he had healed once out of kindness and compassion and how much they had blessed and loved him in return. He remembered their little acts of generosity, sparing him a few coins, a bundle of vegetables from their garden in return for the water. When did he become so selfish and greedy that he would neglect the people who had needed him the most? The old man had taken back his powers when he sensed Ravi had misused the gift.

Never mind, Ravi smiled to himself. He would use the money he had received for the water to help bring a real doctor to the village, someone who would help the people with his knowledge of medicines and diseases, so that they need not wait for a magician to cure them of their illnesses.

From that day onwards Ravi filled his pitcher with ordinary water from the stream and carried it back carefully to his little store and waited for the old man. Maybe one day he would be back, but till then, Ravi was determined to bring a real medicine man to his village.

———

Ajji finished her story and looked around at the four little faces around her. Raghu was deep in thought. Ajji smiled at him. Then the children shouted, 'Ajji, tell one more story!' 'Ah ha,' Ajji said, 'too many stories a day are not good either. One laddoo is very sweet, very delicious but if you eat laddoos all the time it's no fun. Go and play outside. Tomorrow I will tell you another story.' With that she got up and went to the kitchen to supervise the dinner.

Kavery and the Thief

The children had gone with their Ajja to the paddy fields that morning. They were all city kids and did not know a thing about farming! On the way, Anand was surprised to see a bird's nest on top of the tree. He said to Ajja, 'I wonder how birds decide where and how to make their nests!' Ajja said, 'The straw in the nest is from the paddy field. Do you know, farming helps human beings as well as birds?' Krishna replied, 'Ajja, I thought wheat and rice can be just plucked from trees, like mangoes. But today I realized there is so much work in farming.'

That afternoon, after lunch, when they gathered around Ajji for the day's story, she looked sharply at the children. They had enjoyed learning about farming activities like cleaning seeds and separating the straw from paddy. In the city everything came from the supermarket, but here they had seen how things were really produced.

Ajji said, 'Farming is very important. If farmers do not grow any food, then what will we all eat?'

Anand said thoughtfully, 'If farmers do such important work, why are they so poor?'

'That's true, my dear,' Ajji sighed, fanning herself. 'Of course there are rich farmers too, people who own lots of land. But many in our country till small pieces of land, and so make less money.'

Then seeing the kids' crestfallen faces, she put down her fan, sat up and said, 'But I can tell you of a poor farmer woman who did not remain very poor! All due to her sharp wit!'

'Tell Ajji! Do tell!' the kids yelled. So Ajji started her story.

———

Kavery's lazy husband annoyed her no end. There she was working like a donkey in the fields, ploughing and watering and tending a hard, dry piece of land, while her husband snored away happily at home! Why, once when a stranger came asking for some food and water, he just pointed towards the kitchen and went back to sleep. The stranger, thankfully, was an honest man and took only enough for himself and his horse. Not that there was much to steal in

Kavery's little house. They were poor farmers with only a patch of land where nothing seemed to grow. Somehow Kavery tilled the land, did some odd jobs in the neighbourhood, and made ends meet.

The land was right next to a temple. On some days her husband would come along with her on the pretext of helping her, but no sooner would her back be turned than she would find him stretched out near the temple courtyard gossiping with passing villagers.

One day, as she was working in the field, trying to dig up the ground so she could sow some seeds, a thin man with a big moustache appeared beside her. He was a thief, and up to no good. Kavery of course did not know this. She greeted him politely and went back to her work. Now the thief wanted to steal the coins that were given as offerings in the temple and perhaps even the ornaments on the idol. The only way into the temple was by digging his way in from Kavery's land. But how could he do anything there, with this tough, no-nonsense woman working away?

Guessing Kavery was hard up for money, he whispered to her, 'Sister, why are you working so hard on this barren land? I will give you one thousand rupees, sell it to me.'

Kavery raised her eyebrows, why did he want to buy the land for so much money? Surely something was wrong?

The thief sensed she was not about to sell it to him, so he raised his price: 'A thousand and fifty? No? Two thousand? No again? FIVE THOUSAND? No?'

Kavery kept shaking her head. She did not like this odd-looking man who was offering her so much of money for the field. Clearly he had some evil plans. Finally, to keep him quiet, she made up a story. 'I will never sell this land. You see, it belonged to my ancestors. Now we are poor, but I am told that once our family was very rich. Though we lost a lot of our money, much of it was also buried here, in this field by one ancestor, to keep it safe from robbers. Then people forgot about it for years and years. My husband found a clue to the location of the hidden treasure just a few days back. Why do you think I am digging this hard earth? Not to sow seeds, oh no, that's just what everyone thinks. I am actually looking for hidden treasure!'

The thief was stunned. He felt this woman was really innocent, giving such important information to a stranger. He thought, why should I not take advantage of this situation? Here he was, hoping to steal a few coins from the temple, and this woman was telling him about hidden treasure! He replied in a very humble way, 'Yes sister, I understand; after all it is your family treasure. Only you should get it.' He pretended to walk away, and went and hid himself a little way down the road.

Night fell; Kavery packed up her tools and headed home. The temple too emptied out and the priest locked it up for the night. Then at midnight, when all was quiet and the night creatures were coming out of their homes, the thief crept into the field.

All night he dug and dug and dug, looking for treasure, but of course there was no sign of it as there never had been any treasure to begin with! By the time dawn broke he realized Kavery had made a fool of him and all he could do now was get away from the field fast.

When Kavery reached the field she grinned to herself. Just as she had expected, the thief had spent the night digging up the land nicely for her. All she needed to do now was sow the seeds. She worked hard in the field for the next few months and managed to grow a good crop. She sold those and finally they had some money. With a part of this money Kavery bought some jewellery.

Many months later, the thief decided to show his face in the village again. He was careful to disguise himself, though. He trimmed his long moustaches, tied a colourful turban and pretended to be a travelling salesman. No sooner had he stepped into the village than he saw Kavery going about her work. But what is this . . . Instead of the simple, unadorned lady he saw last year, she was now wearing jewellery which looked as though it had been in the family for years! Surely she must have located that missing treasure finally! He was determined to look in her house and find the rest of her money and treasure.

That night, he appeared at Kavery's house and said to her husband, 'I am a traveller and don't have a place to spend the night. Please give me shelter for the night.'

Kavery's husband agreed immediately. Kavery, however, glimpsed the man from inside the house and saw through his disguise. She knew he must be planning some robbery, so she said in a loud voice, making sure the visitor heard her, 'Oh dear, your dear aunt is all alone at night and has asked us to come stay with her. You know how the dark scares her when your uncle is not there. Come, let us go there for the night.' Then lowering her voice a bit, yet making sure she was heard clearly, she continued, 'Don't worry about the jewels. I have hidden them in little holes in the house walls. No one will suspect the hiding spot.' Then she came out and in her normal voice told the thief, 'Brother, you can sleep in the veranda. The house will be locked. Here is some food and water for you. We will come tomorrow morning.' The thief smiled to himself at Kavery's foolishness.

Her husband meanwhile stared at her with an open mouth, wondering which aunt and what jewels she was talking about. When she firmly walked off, he followed obediently.

The thief could not believe his luck. He had the entire night to comb through the house, tap all the walls and look for the hidden stash of gold ornaments. So he started. Tap tap tap. Kick, punch and shove. He prowled and he tapped, he kicked and he pushed the walls, hoping to spot the jewels. Finally he tore down all the walls. But of course there was nothing he could find. Exhausted he fell asleep and woke only with the crowing of the cock as the sun rose. Quickly he found his little bundle of things and ran off. Within minutes Kavery and her husband returned.

'Oh Kavery, see what the bad man has done to our house! You gave him food and shelter and made me come with you leaving the man alone in the night,' her husband wailed. But Kavery was smiling! Then she broke into peals of laughter and said, 'Don't worry. I had planned this all along. You see, I saved money from our last crop to rebuild the house. I needed to call in some labourers to help tear it down, but our guest has done it for us! Now we can make a larger house for ourselves, just the way we always wanted.'

The whole village heard the story and started marvelling at her intelligence. Many months flew by. The thief was burning to take revenge. How dare that village woman trick him, that too not once but twice! He realized that she was very clever.

One day, he dressed up as a bangle seller and started wandering in the village. Kavery spotted him and knew who he was at once. She said to her friends who were crowding around the bangle seller, 'Oh dear, I would have loved to get some for myself. But ever since that good-for-nothing thief tried to steal all our money by tearing down our house, I have hidden everything in a little hole in a tree in the woods.'

'Which tree?' her friends asked.

'Oh no, I am not saying which tree, but it is at last safe and sound out in the forest.'

The thief looked at her. Yes Kavery was wearing an ordinary sari with no ornaments at all.

Her friends turned around in astonishment at the crash with which the bangle seller flung down his collection of bangles and made off for the forest. Only Kavery watched with a grin on her face.

Out in the forest, the thief searched high and low for the jewels. He climbed trees, poked around in bushes, got bitten, scratched and growled at, but he would not give up. The jewels were there somewhere and he had to find them.

So that is where we will leave him, prowling around in the forest, looking for money and gold that don't belong to him. Everyone praised Kavery for her quick wit in ridding the village of the thief.

She continued to work hard and made more money from her farming and became a rich old lady. Even her husband was shamed into giving up his lazy ways and helping her. As for the thief, who knows, perhaps he is still in that forest, looking for what was never his. Now if only he had learnt to work hard like Kavery—he would have been as rich!

———

The children laughed and laughed when the story was over. 'The poor thief!' Meenu and Krishna giggled. 'Maybe he got eaten by a tiger!'

Ajji grinned. 'See,' she told Anand, 'sometimes with a bit of luck and lots of pluck, people can change any situation in which they find themselves!'

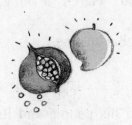

Who Was the
Happiest of Them All?

Meenu was upset. She pouted and sulked and would not talk to Ajji. But how can any child be angry with Ajji for very long? Their grandmother was just too loving and affectionate for anyone to not tell her what was wrong.

'Ajji, it's been three days, and you have not told a story about a king yet!' Meenu grumbled.

Ajji nodded. 'It's true, Meenu. That was my fault; I should have told you a story about a king right away!'

'And I want a good, nice king, who does good, nice things for his people—not horrible things like punishing them and jailing them,' Meenu sat straight and demanded.

'All right, dear. Here's a king, just as you wanted . . .'

And Ajji began her story.

—

King Amrit loved his people and looked after the affairs of his kingdom well. His minister, Chandan, was a wise man who helped the king in his work tirelessly.

One day, King Amrit and Chandan were taking a walk on the terrace of the palace. The terrace offered beautiful views of the surroundings, and they could see far into the distance. They spotted the weekly market from up there, with people in colourful clothes buying and selling all kinds of things. There was plenty to buy and people had money to buy too. There were no poor people to be seen anywhere. The king watched with a smile on his face. He was delighted to see the prosperity of his kingdom. Like any good ruler he was happy when his people were happy.

He turned to Chandan and said, 'See how contented my people are. But I want to check this first-hand by talking to them. Tomorrow, summon people from all walks of life to the court, and I will ask them myself how they are doing.' Chandan was used to the king's strange requests, so he nodded and went off to carry out this order.

The next day, the king arrived in court humming a happy tune to himself. Seeing all the people gathered there waiting for him, he was even more pleased. He cleared his throat and said in a loud voice, 'I have called you here to ask you a very important question. As your king, I need to know if all of you are contented. Do you have enough for your needs? Do you know anyone who is not happy about anything?'

The citizens looked at each other, thought for a while and slowly one by one they came forward to answer. One after the other they all said how happy they were—their kitchens had enough food, their trades and businesses were doing well, the king had made them feel safe. The farmers had grown good crops and the rivers and ponds were full of fish. What more could they ask for?

The king became more and more pleased as he heard this. Only Chandan, his minister, watched and heard everything with a frown on his face. Why? What was wrong? Soon he walked up to the king and whispered something in his ear. King Amrit's eyebrows rose up in astonishment. Surely, Chandan could not be serious! But he looked at the minister's face and found no trace of this being a joke.

He turned back to the court and made a most unusual announcement. 'I am delighted that all of you have said you are happy. But I want to test this. Tomorrow, I want all the happy people of this kingdom to come and meet me in the royal gardens. But I have a condition. All of you will have to enter the garden from the main gate, walk across and meet me by the gate at the rear of the garden. I will wait for you there. When you enter the garden you will be given a sack each and you can pick whatever fruits or flowers your heart desires.'

An excited buzz broke out among the crowd. It sounded like a lot of fun. No one was usually allowed to enter the king's special garden. He had planted trees from all over the world in that garden and it was said to be filled with all kinds of beautiful and strange plants.

Right on time the next day, everyone gathered at the gate of the garden. At the time the king had told them, the guards opened the gates and handed out the sacks. Men, women and children started roaming around the beautiful garden. They spotted juicy apples and plump mangoes hanging from trees. They picked these till they saw ripe pomegranates bursting with juice, grapes and colourful flowers no one had seen before. People went about picking whatever they wished for and filling their sacks with them.

But as they walked further into the garden it became wilder, more like a forest, and there they saw trees laden with apples of gold, mangoes of silver and flowers studded with gems and jewels!

Everyone emptied their sacks of the fruits they had collected earlier and started madly filling them up with these precious fruits and flowers. They all forgot that they had said they had more than enough for their needs at home. Greed took over their minds and all they could think about was adding more and more valuables to their sacks. The fruits which they had picked earlier, and had tasted to be as sweet as nectar, now lay in heaps around the garden—forgotten and left to rot.

Then with their sacks filled right to the top, the citizens made their way to the rear gate of the garden where the king was waiting. But what was this? To their astonishment they found a raging stream stopping their way. Water gushed down from behind some rocks and rushed over pebbles and big boulders through the garden. The stream was narrow, but the current was strong. There were no boats to take the people across. Clearly, the only way was to swim. But how could they swim with such heavy sacks filled with gold and silver apples and other fruits?

The people stood by the stream for a long time scratching their heads. Then one young man did what they all knew needed to be done. He simply abandoned his sack by the stream, waded into the water, then swam across to the other side. Slowly the others too followed suit. Sadly, some wailing in distress, they left their sacks filled with what they had thought was the riches of a lifetime, and dived into the stream. Then they walked up to their king—wet, unhappy and angry.

King Amrit and Chandan watched them trudge up in their soaking clothes. Chandan had a small smile on his lips, while the king looked sad. When they had assembled in front of him, he said, 'When I asked you yesterday if you were happy with your lives, all of you said you were contented and did not need anything more. Yet, today I can see the sadness in your faces when you had to leave behind the riches you had gathered in my garden. If you were really happy with your lives, why did you gather the jewel fruits, and why are you so sad now?'

Everyone looked down, ashamed at their behaviour. Only the young man who was the first to cross the stream after leaving his sack behind seemed to be unconcerned. Chandan spotted his cheerful face in the crowd and beckoned him forward. Then he asked, 'Tell me, are you not sad you had to leave behind so much of wealth that suddenly came your way?'

The man said, 'I didn't pick the jewelled fruits and flowers. I had picked some of the lovely, tasty fruits and had eaten my fill of them. In my sack I had kept some others for my little daughter who is at home. I had thought she would enjoy these tasty apples and mangoes. But when I saw there was no other way to go across the stream, I did not think twice about leaving my sack by the river. My little girl can get tasty fruits from some other garden too! But I am so happy the king let us all wander around his garden,

looking at the trees and plants and animals. He is a great king for having created this place of beauty, and it was a pleasure walking around there.'

Finally a smile appeared on King Amrit's face. Chandan turned to him and said, 'Your Majesty, I hope you now realize that people's contentment does not end with having enough food or money. They also need to be truly happy inside. Only then will they not be swayed when they gain or lose wealth. That is a lesson that everyone—whether a king or a commoner—needs to remember.'

The king nodded, as did his subjects. This was a lesson they would not forget in a hurry!

———

'Did you like the story, Meenu?' Raghu asked.

'Oh yes,' Meenu nodded. 'But I liked the minister more than the king!'

'That's true, Meenu,' Ajji agreed. 'Kings did need intelligent ministers to show them the right path sometimes. Remember Akbar had Birbal, and Krishnadevaraya had Tenali Rama? Why just kings, we all need someone to tell us if what we are doing is wrong. It could be our parents, grandparents, teachers or even our best friend. The important thing is to listen to them and change our ways when needed.'

The Enchanted Scorpions

What an exciting morning the children had had that day! Ajja had asked for their help in cleaning up his old storeroom. Ajja loved to keep all kinds of old things in that room, much to Ajji's annoyance. She firmly believed the room was the principle attraction for all the cockroaches, mice, termites and other such bugs in the house. Every summer holiday the children spent a day clearing out the room, exclaiming over all the treasures they had unearthed. Ajja even let them keep some of the odds and ends they found. That didn't please their mothers too much though!

Today they had found an old wooden box. It was a big box, beautifully carved all over with flowers and vines and leaves. Inside, it had little compartments to keep all manner of things. Now these compartments were empty, but Raghu, who had been reading *Treasure Island*, imagined that once these were full of gold and silver coins, gems as big as eggs and all kinds of fantastic jewels.

After examining the box thoroughly, the children decided that the day's story had to be about lost treasure. Ajji, who knew a story about anything under the sun, started right away.

Siddharth was a young, good-natured merchant. Looking for work, he arrived in a village. He liked the people of the village so much that he decided to use all his savings, buy a house and live there forever. While searching for a house, he met Uday.

Uday was a poor man. His family had once been extremely wealthy landowners but were now not so well off. Uday was looking to sell his old family mansion in order to pay off his family's loans.

Siddharth loved the house Uday showed him and bought it immediately. Then he set about repairing the mansion, which was in ruins. As he dug out the old flooring, he found a sealed box buried underground. When he opened it, to his surprise, he saw it was filled with scorpions. He flung the box away in fright.

That evening, he went to visit the wisest man in the village and asked him about the box of scorpions. The wise man thought for a while, then said, 'Perhaps Uday's ancestors hid some money in that box and buried it, to be used when someone in the family needed the money. Over the years they must have forgotten about the existence of the box.'

Siddharth was still puzzled. 'But the box contained scorpions,' he said, 'not money.'

The old man smiled. 'The box is protected by an old spell. If it is opened by anyone other than a family member, it will appear as if it is swarming with scorpions. Only a true family member will be able to see that the box contains money.'

Siddharth was sad to hear this story. He remembered the tears that had sprung up in Uday's eyes as he had looked back at his ancestral house for one last time before leaving the village. If only he had known about the hidden treasure, he would not have had to sell the house. When Siddharth reached home, he decided to keep the box safely till someone from Uday's family came to claim it. To make sure that the box was taken only by a true descendant of Uday's family, he took four scorpions from the box and hung them in four corners of his newly opened shop.

All his customers would comment when they entered the shop. 'Siddharth, are you mad? Why have you hung dangerous insects in your shop? Do you want to scare away shoppers?'

But Siddharth would only smile. He knew his goods were the best for miles around, and people would come to shop at his store, scorpions or not. Gradually the shop came to be known as the Scorpion Shop and the villagers laughed at him behind his back. But Siddharth did not care.

Many years passed. Siddharth was now a middle-aged man with a wife and children and enough money. But he had one regret. No one had come to claim that box.

One day, a young boy walked into the shop and said, 'Sir, I have heard from many people in the village that you are wealthy and often help those in need. I had to stop going to school because I could no longer pay my fees. Could you please lend me some money so I can finish my studies?'

Siddharth shook his head sadly. 'The villagers have exaggerated about my wealth,' he said. 'Yes, I am earning enough, but not so much that I can help you or lend you money, though I would have loved to do so.'

The boy flared up in anger when he heard this. 'Sir, if you do not want to help me, please say so openly. Why do you lie? You have so much money that you don't know what to do with it. Why else have you hung gold coins in the four corners of your shop? Surely you can spare some coins to help a poor student like me.'

Siddharth stared at him in astonishment. 'Wh-what? What did you just say?' he asked, his eyes bulging in excitement.

'I said if you don't want to help . . .' the boy repeated.

'Yes, yes, I heard that,' Siddharth cut him short. 'But what did you say after that, about the gold coins in my shop?'

The boy now looked at Siddharth doubtfully, afraid that perhaps this excited old man was a bit mad. 'I said you are so wealthy that you have hung gold coins in the four corners of the shop. There they are, for the world to see!' And the boy pointed to what appeared to Siddharth as four writhing scorpions.

Siddharth gave a happy whoop of laughter. He rushed forward and hugged the boy.

'Are you related to Uday Kamalakar? Did your family ever live in this village?' he nearly shouted into the boy's ears.

The young man stepped back in alarm. Perhaps this rich man was mad and dangerous after all. 'Y-yes, my name is Uday. I was named after my grandfather. His family lived here for many generations. Then, when they fell on hard times, my grandfather sold his old house and moved. He never recovered from the grief of having to sell his ancestral property and died heartbroken.'

Siddharth wiped away the tears from his eyes. 'Wait here my son,' he said. Rushing to his house, he came back with the old box and gave it to the young boy. 'Go on, open it and tell me what you see,' he chuckled.

The boy opened the box and his eyes nearly fell out of his head. For he held in his hands more treasure than he could dream about in his wildest fantasies. The box was filled with gold and silver coins and jewels!

He looked up in astonishment at Siddharth, who was grinning broadly. 'Yes, it belongs to you,' Siddharth explained. 'I have held it safe for many years, hoping someone from Uday's family will come to claim it. Your troubles are now over. Go home, use the wealth of your ancestors judiciously and do well in life.'

Then he told the boy the story of how he had found the box which appeared to be filled with scorpions to anyone who did not belong to Uday's family.

Uday was amazed when he heard the story. He offered Siddharth half his wealth in gratitude. But Siddharth would hear none of it. 'This is yours,' he insisted. 'Go, enjoy your life.'

Uday went away with the box, and all his life he remembered the funny, honest old man who had kept his wealth safely for him.

'How lovely, Ajji!' Krishna gasped. 'If only we had such a shopkeeper in this town!' All the children agreed that that would have been such fun. Ajji laughed at their dreamy faces. Then she shooed them out to play in the garden. And do you know what they played till late in the evening? Treasure hunt, of course!

The Horse Trap

The next day, there was a surprise summer shower. The land smelled beautiful. The thirsty earth had soaked in every drop of rainwater. The children had been very busy shifting the puppies and kittens, who were roaming in the back and front yards, into the house so that they did not get drenched in the rain. Their respective mothers were very busy shifting the pappadams left to dry on the terrace. Summer is the season when, under Ajji's leadership, pickles and pappadams were made.

Meenu started a calculation. 'Everyone needs at least five pappadams per day. For the next one month 600 pappadams will be needed. Tomorrow our neighbour Vishnu Kaka's three grandchildren are coming. They will also eat with us these tasty pappadams. We may have to keep five per head . . . That means Ajji has to prepare 600 + 50 pappadams.' When Ajji listened to Meenu's mathematics, she laughed and said, 'Don't calculate that way. It may be true today that we will all eat five pappadams a day, but this may not be true for every day. After eating pappadams for three days, one may get bored. There is a wedding in my brother's house and we all might go there. So we may not eat any pappadam those days. The way you are calculating, reminds me of the man who calculated the number of horses, once in England . . .'

All the children immediately gathered around her. 'Oh Ajji, you must tell us this story of how the horses were counted.'

So Ajji had to stop what she was doing right there and tell them the story.

Many many years ago, in England, there lived a great thinker and scholar called George Smith. He thought a lot about how it would be in the future, and advised the prime minister about many things. He researched how many people would live in the country in twenty years' time, he calculated how many schools, hospitals and roads needed to be built, or how much food needed to be grown or bought from other places to feed all these people.

His calculations helped the government immensely in planning for the future.

George often needed to visit the prime minister's office to talk to him about some new project and advise him. One day, the prime minister had invited him for a meeting, so he hopped into his horse carriage and set off for the office. Now George was always deep in thought and rarely noticed what was happening around him. Today too he sat in his carriage thinking about farms and ships and houses. But suddenly his carriage stopped with a jolt and he was shaken out of his thoughts. There was some commotion on the road and all carriages had stopped around him. Normally George would have just sunk back into his thoughts again, but today something stopped him. A horrible, strong smell. A smell that hung in the air and made you cover your nose with a hanky if you were not a scholar wrapped up in your own world.

Today somehow, George was not able to disconnect himself from what was going on around him. The smell kept wafting into his nose and taking his mind away from the problem he was tackling. He called out to his coachman, 'Hi John, what is this extraordinary smell?'

John the coachman was used to his master's absent-minded ways, and he replied briefly, 'Horse dung.'

Horse dung! Now that was something George had never given a thought to. Somehow, he could now

think of nothing else. Soon his carriage pulled up in front of the prime minister's office. But George kept sitting inside, lost in thought. Finally John tapped on the window to tell his master that they had reached their destination.

George walked to the visitor's room still thinking. He was sitting there, reflecting on horses and their dung, when the prime minister's secretary came to meet him. Now Adam, the secretary, was not as learned as George, but he was very sharp and intelligent. He greeted George and said to him apologetically, 'The PM had to make time for another important meeting, and will be late in seeing you. I hope you don't mind waiting.'

George kept staring out of the window, watching yet more horse-drawn carriages rushing up and down the road. Thinking he had perhaps not heard him, Adam cleared his throat and repeated loudly, 'Mr Smith, the PM . . .'

'Yes, I heard you Adam,' George mumbled.

Worried that this great thinker of the country was in some trouble, Adam asked gingerly, 'Is something bothering you? Perhaps I could help . . .?'

George looked at him excitedly, 'You know, I just looked into the future and realized we will all die in about a hundred years. Our country will be destroyed, our way of life gone forever. And do you know why? All because of horses . . . and their dung!'

Adam stared at George, puzzled. Surely he could not be serious?

George continued, 'See, now we use horses as the principal mode of transport in the country. They are used to draw carriages, in the king's stables, even in the farms.'

Adam nodded. This was true.

'So how many horses are there now? Let's assume that there are 500 rich families who can afford to own a horse carriage. If each family has at least two children and all of them are rich enough to own carriages, that will mean a minimum of two more carriages in a few years. Each carriage would require two horses. So, each rich family would be using four horses at the least. So then there will be

2,000 horses. If you add our king's cavalry, and the number of horses in the farms, the numbers increase substantially.'

Adam nodded. Yes, this sounded true enough, but what was George's point?

'How do we get rid of the dung they generate now?'

Adam answered patiently, 'We dig pits and empty the dung into them.'

George nodded, 'Now that's my point. Imagine the scene a hundred years from now. 2,000 horses would have increased to 400,000, given the way the population is increasing. This will mean more dung! And what will we do with all this dung? Humans will need more space and houses and farming to sustain themselves. Where will we find open land to dig up and bury the dung? It will lie unattended everywhere and cause horrible diseases. If they make their way into the water sources it will be even worse. We will end up poisoning ourselves and our environment. We will become sick, and our country will become poor just by tending to so many sick people, and finally our way of life will just die out—as we all will. All because of horses!'

Adam sat and thought about this for some time. George's thoughts and the grim picture he had painted of the future was scary indeed. But . . . here Adam's practical thinking kicked in; what if things did not work exactly the way George was seeing it? He turned to his friend and said, 'Mr Smith, you are not taking into account one very important bit into your calculations—the ability humans have to innovate and adapt. Many years ago there were no carts or carriages, we went everywhere by foot. Then once we started domesticating animals we realized we could use them for transport too. But do you think humans will rest with this achievement? Who knows, in a hundred years what other modes of transport we would have invented so that we may not require horse for transport at all. Perhaps we will even be able to fly like birds!'

George never solved this problem in his lifetime. Neither did Adam live to see how true his thoughts about the future had been. Man went on to invent so many new ways of moving from place to place that

horses are no longer used in the numbers they once were. James Watt invented the steam engine, which led to the invention of railways. Then cars were invented by Karl F. Benz and became widely used in cities for transport. Finally the Wright brothers showed that humans could fly—in aeroplanes! With all these great inventions, the horse and other animal-drawn carts and carriages are now a thing of the past.

Truly, if man did not innovate and experiment, our species would have died out—just like George had predicted!

Everyone was very happy this story. They all teased Meenu. 'You are the George Smith of our house. Who knows one day nobody will eat pappadams and Amma may not prepare that many pappadams. We may even buy directly from the shops if it is a small number.'

Meenu felt very embarrassed. She hid her face with a pillow. Ajji said, 'Don't make fun of her. Foresight is very important. If you don't have foresight, then you will land up in trouble like Ramu.'

'Who is Ramu?' the children immediately asked Ajji.

'I will tell the story of Ramu only tomorrow.' And Ajji bustled off. The children knew she would tell only one story a day, so they eagerly waited for the next day and to hear Ramu's story.

A Treasure for Ramu

Vishnu Kaka's grandchildren had come to visit him. Vishnu Kaka was a very good friend of Ajja's. They had lived next door to each other for years. Unfortunately, his wife Vasanthi Kaki had died a few years back. Though there was a cook, his grandchildren, Sharan, Suma and Divya, always preferred to eat in Ajji's house, which Ajji also welcomed.

With seven hungry children to feed, Ajji realized telling a story would be a good way to keep them quiet till the food got cooked. Ajji started the story while peeling the cucumbers.

47

Did you know that sometimes even the gods in heaven can get into an argument? That's what happened once when Lakshmi, the goddess of wealth, found herself cornered by all the other gods. Together, they accused her of one thing—that she never stayed in one place for too long! 'No sooner are you comfortably settled in one house, do you decide to leave it, and off you go elsewhere!' they said to her.

Lakshmi sniffed and said, 'That's not true. I stay in a house as long as I am welcome. If people think ahead, work sincerely and spend money wisely, I stay with them forever. Unfortunately often when I am in one place for a while, people behave strangely, and I have no choice but to leave.'

The other gods pooh-poohed this and refused to believe her. Poor Lakshmi decided she needed to show them proof of what she had just said. Here is what she did to show that she was correct. Remember, many human years make only a second in god years. So what took years to happen on earth, the gods could see in only a few minutes.

Ramu and Rani were farmers. They worked hard in their fields and earned enough money to feed their children and meet their other needs. They were not rich and sometimes had to make do with fewer new clothes and not very nice food.

One day, Rani was digging a corner of her garden in order to plant a tree. As she dug deeper, there was a loud clang! Her shovel had hit something metallic hidden underground. Excited, she dug faster, till she pulled out a large metal box. When she opened it she could not believe her eyes. It was filled with gold and silver jewels! For a while Rani stood dumbstruck. Then she did a happy whoop and ran home with the box under her arm.

'Ramu, Ramu, see what I found buried in our garden!' she yelled.

Ramu was writing up the accounts for the month, and for a while paid no attention to his wife. Only when she came up to him and did a happy jig around him did he look up. Imagine how his mouth fell open in surprise when he saw the box of jewels.

Soon Ramu and Rani were the richest people in the village. They stopped going to work—after all, what was the need, they told each other. Why work in the hot sun when they had piles of money at home? They left their small cottage and moved into the biggest house in the village. They had servants who worked day and night doing every small job so the two did not need to lift even a finger. There was a cook who cooked delicious meals, a person to serve it, another just to clean shoes and one person to even fan Ramu as he sat on his bed the whole day and gossiped with his newfound friends.

Then Ramu decided village life was too boring and they moved to the big city. There they had another big house, more servants and lots of fun at various parties. Slowly they forgot the good things that had once made them a well-loved family. They forgot to work hard, to help others in their need, or to just be nice people. They thought that with money they could buy anything, including respect. They behaved rudely to others. They spent more and more money on clothes and parties, and as they did no work at all, the money started dwindling. They started borrowing from others which they soon could not pay back.

One day, Ramu looked sadly at his account book. It was now filled with numbers that showed he only needed to pay others; there was hardly anything left for himself. In a heavy voice he called out to his wife, 'Rani dear, the good days are over. I think we forgot to be the kind of people Goddess Lakshmi likes. She has gone elsewhere, and we are left with nothing.'

Rani stood silently for a while, then replied, 'Never mind, Ramu. We have learnt our lesson. I now think of the days when I would work all day long and go to sleep a tired person and sleep soundly. I would fall into a deep slumber as soon as I lay down on the bed. Now I lie awake all night wondering which sari to wear the next day and what to do with our money. I am too fat to even dig, like I did when I found the treasure!'

Ramu smiled and hugged his wife. 'We'll go back to our village, and to our old ways. We will work hard like we did once, and we will help everyone around us. Maybe that will make Lakshmi come back to us one day. And even if she doesn't, we will try and be happy with what we have.'

So Ramu and his family went back to their old home. And do you know what? They did live happily ever after!

⸻

The gods watched what was happening with Ramu and Rani from the heavens as Lakshmi entered and then left their house. They had to agree with her—if the people of the house she entered became nasty, then what could she do except leave, and hope they saw the error of their ways?

The Donkey and the Stick

Ajji was on an outing with her daughter and daughter-in-law, Sumati and Subhadra. One lived in Bangalore and the other in Mumbai. They were returning the next day as they had used up all the leaves their offices had given. The children would remain at Shiggaon though, with their grandparents. Everyone was looking forward to this stage of the holidays. The children because there would be no parents telling them what to do, to Ajji's delicious food and to fun outings with Ajja. The grandparents too were looking forward to having the children to themselves. The rest of the year it was only the two of them in the house.

As Ajji walked with the two younger women, they talked about how difficult it was for them to manage their office work and the children. Ajji listened silently. Then Sumati said, 'But they are so good when they are with you, Amma. How do you manage them so well?' Subhadra nodded. 'I have read so many books and articles to find out about this, but nothing works the way it is written in books.'

Now Ajji said, 'Do not always go by what you read in books. Learn to use your life's experiences, read between the lines.' Then she grinned and said, 'Otherwise you will become like the people in the story about the donkey and the stick!'

Sumati and Subhadra forgot they were at the temple and clamoured together, 'What is this story? Tell us!' Ajji shook her head. 'Now you are behaving like children. But you are my children after all. All right, come join us at night when I tell today's story.'

That night the two mothers were the first to appear to listen to the stories. The children were surprised to see their mums, and Ajji started her story.

***

Aruna Marg was a busy road. It connected a number of villages to each other and many people, animals and carts used it every day. Walking along that road, a group of students discovered a rock which no one had bothered to look at in many years. 'Look!' they told each other in excitement, 'there is something written on the rock. What can it mean?'

They called out to their teacher. When they examined the rock carefully, they found the markings were actually little drawings. One showed a stick, and the other a donkey.

By now a large crowd had gathered. Everyone was puzzled. What could these strange drawings mean, they asked, scratching their heads. They decided to go to the ashram of a wise sage nearby and ask him. But when they trooped into the ashram, they found to their disappointment that the sage had gone on a long pilgrimage. Only his young disciple was there, looking after the cows and calves.

They asked the disciple if he could throw some light on the strange drawings. Now this young man was not very bright. But like many foolish people he loved to put on an air of learning and pretend to be very clever. He examined the drawings carefully and minutely. Then he proclaimed, 'It is very simple. This is the drawing of a magic stick. The man with the stick is the hero of this place. He died protecting this village centuries back. Each person using this road must worship the rock and make an offering to it. The one who ignores it will become a donkey!'

The villagers were astonished to hear this strange explanation. But they were devout people and on that very day they set up a shrine around the rock. They installed the foolish disciple as head priest in charge of taking offerings from passing travellers. The disciple was pleased with his brainwave. Of course he did not know what the silly drawings meant, but he no longer had to run after calves and get kicked by angry cows in the ashram! He could sit by the rock the whole day, taking his pick of the offerings to the rock and mutter a few mumbo-jumbo prayers.

His happiness lasted a few months—till the wise old sage returned to the ashram. The old sage was annoyed to find his disciple missing and his beloved animals roaming around, uncared for. Then he looked into the distance and saw a large crowd gathered by the road. He went to investigate, and found his missing disciple there, looking happy and well fed, busy accepting offerings for a rock. He stood watching for a while. Then he walked up to the rock and closely examined the pictures. Without saying a word, he picked up a stout iron rod and, to the astonishment of the gathered crowd, started moving the rock. Many came forward to help him and when they had been able to move the rock, they found a pot of gold under it!

The sage said to the people gathered around him: 'The pictures meant you had to move the rock with an iron rod and find the hidden money. If you didn't, you were all like donkeys. You should not follow rituals and the words of others blindly. Think for yourselves and understand why you are doing what you do. If you had given this some thought, you

would have recovered this treasure many months ago. Instead, you wasted your time and money making offerings to a rock and helping this greedy disciple of mine become fat and make fools of you. This treasure belongs to all of us. Let's use it to keep this road in good repair so everyone can use it and go about their work in peace.'

The villagers hung their heads in shame for they realized how foolish they had been. As for the disciple, he had to clean the cowsheds for many months to atone for his greed.

'What's in It for Me?'

Ajja told Anand, 'Will you go fetch my clothes from the dhobi?' Anand was reading a book, and said without looking up, 'Then what will you give me?' Ajja smiled and said, 'I will give you nothing. Why should I give you anything? You are a part of the family.' Anand looked up now. 'Oh! But that is not true in our house,' he declared. 'Whenever my dad tells me to do some work, I ask for a reward and he gives it to me.' Ajja was surprised. 'Let me talk to your father. The joy of helping someone itself is a reward. This is not right.'

'Dad is a big officer in a bank. Can he make mistakes?' asked Krishna with great surprise.

'He may be an officer in the bank but at home he is your father and my son, and I will talk to him. If you go on like this you will become like "Mushika".'

'What's a "Mushika"?' asked Sharan.

Ajja looked around. There was no sign of Ajji. Probably churning out some last-minute masala powder for the mothers to take back with them. He looked pleased. 'Today I will tell you a story. Of a Mushika and what happens if you want to be paid for every little thing.'

Mushika the mouse walked jauntily down the road, whistling a happy tune to himself. There had been a storm earlier in the day which had gotten rid of the summer heat. He had just eaten a big, juicy mango that had fallen in the storm, so his tummy was full and he was as pleased as punch. On the road, he saw a twig, also fallen from the tree above in the storm. Now a mouse will store and keep anything, hoping it will be of use one day. So Mushika picked up the twig in his mouth and set off.

A little ahead he met a potter. The potter was sitting with his head in hands. Why? Because his oven had been drenched in the rain and now he did not have enough dry wood to light it again. How would he bake his pots and sell them?

As the potter sat wailing in front of his house, Mushika walked up and watched him for some time. 'Wossh up, brother?' he asked with the twig still clutched in his mouth.

At first the potter paid no attention to the strange talking mouse. Then when Mushika asked him again and again, he told the little creature why he was crying. Mushika nodded, kept the twig aside and said, 'See, this twig has dried in the wind and can be used to light your kiln. I'll happily give it you Brother Potter, but what's in it for me?'

The potter thought hard, and deciding that a little mouse could not ask for much, said, 'I will give whatever you ask for.'

In a flash Mushika replied, 'Then give me that large pumpkin that is lying in the corner of the room.'

The potter was astonished—how can a mouse carry a pumpkin? Besides, he had been looking forward to the lovely pumpkin curry his wife would make for him that night. 'Choose something else, little mouse,' he urged. But Mushika was stubborn—the pumpkin for the twig, or nothing.

So the potter gave Mushika the pumpkin. The mouse was delighted. He had made a mighty human do what he wanted! He left the pumpkin near the potter's house saying he would collect it soon and set off down the road again.

Further ahead, a milkman was sitting by his cows, shaking his head. 'What's up, Brother Milkman?' asked a tiny voice. To his astonishment the man saw a mouse with bright eyes peeping up at him.

Sadly he shook his head some more, then said, 'The storm scared my cows and they are refusing to give me milk. What will I sell today and what will my family eat?'

'Spicy pumpkin curry—if you want!'

'Surely you are joking, my friend. I have ten people at home. Where will I get a pumpkin large enough to feed everyone?'

'Just walk back the way I came. You will reach a potter's house. Right beside that I have left a pumpkin. That's mine, and you can have it. But what's in it for me, Brother?'

The milkman shrugged and said, 'Whatever you want.' Like the potter he thought, what can a mouse want?

Mushika said, 'Then give me a cow.'

'Are you mad? A pumpkin for a cow? Whoever has heard such a thing?'

'It's that or nothing, my friend,' replied Mushika firmly. So the milkman went and got the large pumpkin and gave one cow to the mouse.

A big cow with large horns that listened to what he commanded! Mushika the mouse could not believe his luck. Off he went, seated on the cow, whistling another happy tune, when he stopped in front of a marriage hall. Why were people standing around looking sad and worried? They should be busy preparing for the marriage feast! Even the bride and groom were standing, with long faces.

'What's up, Brother Groom?' called Mushika, sitting atop his cow.

The groom replied gloomily, 'There's no milk to prepare the wedding kheer. How will the wedding feast be complete without the dessert?'

Mushika grinned. 'Worry not. Here, take this cow, she is now happy and will give you milk. But what's in it for me, Brother?'

The groom was very happy and said, 'Why, you can have whatever you want! You can eat your fill of the feast—sweets, pulao, fruits, whatever your heart desires.' The mouse kept quiet and gave the cow to the wedding party. They milked the cow and had plenty of milk. There was a great wedding feast. After the party was over, the mouse replied in a flash, 'Give me your bride!'

The groom and everyone in the marriage party were astonished at the mouse's cheek. The groom was about to give him a good whack, when his newly wedded bride stopped him. 'You had given him your word that he could have whatever he wants. Let me go with him. I'll teach him such a lesson that he will never try to carry off another human bride again!'

Her husband agreed, so off she went with the mouse.

Mushika scampered ahead, eager to show the bride his home. But what was this, why was she walking so slowly?

'Hurry up, Bride,' he called. 'It's about to rain again.'

The bride replied, 'I am a human, I can't run as fast as you.'

So Mushika had to slow down. By the time they reached his home, which was a little hole under a tree, he was very hungry.

'Cook me a nice meal with lots of grain,' he commanded.

The bride nodded and said, 'Of course, but where is the kitchen, the spices, the oil and the vessels? I am a human after all, I can't cook only grains.'

The mouse realized he was in a real fix having got this useless human back with him. 'Never mind,' he sighed. 'At least come inside the house.'

'Oh, but how will I do that?' wailed the bride. 'I cannot set even a toe inside that hole, it is so small. Where will I sleep tonight?'

'Err, how about under that tree?' Mushika suggested, pointing to another big tree nearby.

'No way,' sniffed the bride. 'It will rain and I will get wet and I will catch a cold then a fever, and I will need a doctor, who will give me bitter medicines . . .' Now she started wailing even louder.

'Shush shush,' Mushika comforted her, thinking he should have agreed to eat his fill of the wedding feast instead of bringing this strange whiny woman back home with him. 'How about you stay in that

temple veranda for the night?' he suggested, pointing to a big temple across the road.

'Oh, but thieves and robbers will come there, and try to snatch away my lovely jewels,' cried the woman. Then suddenly she dried her tears and said, 'What if I call my friends Ram and Shyam to protect me?'

Before Mushika could say anything, she whistled loudly and called, 'Ramu, Shyamu!'

From nowhere a big dog and cat appeared next to her and made as if to eat up Mushika. Oh, how he ran and saved his life by jumping into the safety of his hole.

The bride grinned and went back to her wedding feast with her faithful pets. As for Mushika, he had to go to sleep on an empty stomach that night. 'Tomorrow,' he sighed, 'perhaps there will be another storm.' And went off to sleep.

The Princess' New Clothes

After their mothers went back, Ajji took all the children on a shopping spree. They went to the biggest clothes store in the town. Ajji had filled her purse with notes and told all the seven children, 'Each of you can buy one dress. It is our gift to you. Remember, I have Rs 500 for each of you to buy one dress.'

At the store she chose a nice comfortable chair. The children were allowed to decide which clothes they wanted and in which colour. They could go into the trial room and try them out before buying. After an hour, everybody had whatever they wanted, except Krishna. She had tried on many many dresses but found a fault with all of them. She told Ajii, 'This store does not have anything nice for me. Shall we go to another one?'

'What is wrong with this store? It is a well-known store,' Ajji remarked. But Krishna pouted and complained that she already had the colours and cuts available here, so everyone trooped off to the next shop. There too after a lot of thought finally Krishna chose her dress. Ajji had been watching all this with her typical soft smile. On the way back, as they piled into the taxi, she whispered to Krishna, 'It's good you chose a dress finally. But beware, or else you may turn out to be like that princess . . .'

'Which princess, Ajji?' the children asked.

'The one in the story.' Ajji was now looking out of the window.

'Tell us, oh tell us!'

So Ajji told them the story of the princess who never liked any of her clothes.

The king and queen of Ullas were very sad. No one was attacking them, the subjects were happy, the farmers had grown a bumper crop. Then why were they so sad? Because they longed for a child and did not have one.

One day, they learnt of a place in the forests in the kingdom, where if you prayed hard and well, you were granted your wish. They went there and for many days prayed to the goddess of the forest. Finally their prayers were heard and the goddess appeared before them and asked what they wished for.

The king and queen bowed low and said, 'We wish to have a child.'

'So be it, you will soon have a little girl,' said the goddess, shimmering in the greenery. 'But remember, though she will be a loving child, she will have one flaw. She will love new clothes too much and it will make life difficult for you. Do you still want such a child?'

The king and queen wanted a baby so much they would have agreed to anything. So the goddess granted them their wish and vanished back among the trees.

Soon, as had been said, the queen gave birth to a lovely baby girl. Oh, what a beauty the little thing was, with her jet black hair and thick eyelashes and long toes and fingers. They named her Beena. The kingdom rejoiced in their king's happiness and for a while there was complete joy everywhere.

Beena grew up a child loved by everyone. She became prettier by the day, and with her charming manners and ready laughter, she filled everyone's heart with joy. But, as the goddess had said once, she did have one flaw—she loved new clothes! She loved clothes so much she had to have a new outfit every day. She would even refuse to wear the same clothes twice! Tailors from all over the kingdom and even outside created beautiful, extraordinary clothes for her. Silk, cotton, wool, you name it, and Beena had a dress or sari of that material. Blues, greens, reds, pinks, every colour in nature was present in her wardrobe.

For a while the king and queen were happy to let her have new clothes every day. But soon they realized they were spending all their money and time in finding new tailors and clothes for their daughter! This had to stop.

They coaxed and cajoled and pleaded and scolded, but Beena remained unmoved. Her parents understood this was the flaw the goddess had warned them about, and finally decided to send Beena to the goddess to find a solution.

Beena entered the dark, green forest and waited for the goddess to appear before her. She came in a flash of green light, which lit up everything around her. Folding her hands, Beena told the goddess why she had come.

'I know your problem, my child. I will send you a new outfit every day. It will be unique, its colours and design will delight you. But you should remember one thing: you cannot wear anything else, or exchange these clothes with anyone else. If you ever do that, your life will be miserable.'

Happily Beena agreed to this. After all, why would she be unhappy if she got a new dress every day?

From then on, Beena woke up each morning to find an extraordinary new sari or dress lying by her bed,

ready to be worn. It was a dream come true for her! She enjoyed herself no end, choosing the matching earrings and bangles and shoes and everyone told her how pretty she looked.

Yet after some months the excitement died down. No one remarked when Beena sashayed in wearing another fantastic dress. 'Oh, it's the goddess' gift,' they all said. 'It's not something you or I can ever have,' all her friends said and shrugged and went their way.

Beena grew sadder and sadder. Then one festival day, walking near the river, she noticed a girl wearing a simple cotton sari. There was something about the way the girl walked and how attractive she looked which made everyone turn and stare. Beena noticed how the people were admiring the girl. She was so jealous because no one noticed her beautiful clothes any longer, yet they had such praise for this simply dressed girl. She forgot all about the goddess' warning, went up to the girl and said, 'Will you take my dress and give me your sari in return? It is so lovely that people can't take their eyes off it.'

The girl was astonished. The famous Princess Beena was offering to take her sari, and was giving her a marvellous outfit in exchange! She could not believe her luck and happily gave her sari to Beena. She then wore Beena's dress and went away. No sooner had Beena worn the girl's sari than there was a flash and a bang. Her surroundings changed, and she found herself transported deep inside the forest, in front of the goddess.

'Beena,' the goddess called. 'I had told you that you cannot give away or exchange the clothes I gave you. But you have done just that! I am afraid there is a punishment for not listening to me. I will have to take you away from the world of humans forever.'

Beena looked down in sadness. She thought of her parents' tear-stained faces, the grief of the people in her kingdom who had loved her dearly. Then she spoke aloud, 'I will go away, but do grant me one last wish. Turn me into something that will remind everyone about their beloved princess; something they may even find useful.'

The goddess smiled and turned Beena into a plant. Do you know what plant Beena became? An onion! Have you noticed that the onion has many layers? Those are all the dresses that Beena once wore. And have you noticed your mother's eyes water while she cuts the onion? That is because unknown to ourselves, like all the people in Beena's kingdom, we still shed tears for a beautiful, kind-hearted princess!

After listening to this story, Krishna wailed, 'Ajji, I don't want to be like Beena. I don't want to get turned into an onion! I promise not to fuss over my clothes from now on!'

The Story of Paan

Vishnu Kaka had invited the entire family for dinner. It was a lavish meal with many courses. Everyone ate to the fill, enjoying each dish. After it was over, the children gathered around Kaka as he brought out his big box of paan. They loved watching how Kaka mixed and chose his ingredients to make delicious paans which the grown-ups then ate with blissful looks on their faces.

He explained to the children, 'A paan contains betel leaf, betel nut and lime. But we should use only so much of each ingredient. Only then will it taste good.' All seven children wanted to try this experiment on their own. Some of them chewed on only the leaf, some on the nut, and others on the nut and leaf, or the leaf and only lime. It was true, when the three were not put together, the paan tasted horrible! In fact, Sharan vomited when he added more lime than necessary! Everyone made a beeline for the mirror to check if their tongue was red or not.

Ajji was sitting and chatting with Sharan's mom and watching their antics. Then she called out to them and said, 'Children, by this time you all know that the leaf, nut or lime on their own taste very bad. Even if you put just two together it is no good. Only when you add the three in a perfect combination can a paan be eaten. And that's when you get that red colour in the mouth!'

'Why is that, Ajji? Is there any special meaning?'

'Yes there is a special meaning and I'll tell you the story, which I first heard from my grandmother.'

—

Once upon a time, there were two brothers, Bhanu and Veer. Their parents died when they were young and Bhanu brought up his younger brother with a lot of love and care. When Bhanu was old enough, he married Bharati. She was a gentle, loving person and looked after Veer with as much love as her husband.

When Veer was about twenty years of age, he heard that their king was looking for soldiers to join his army, as there was going to be a war. Veer decided to join the army. Oh, how much his brother and sister-in-law cried and pleaded, telling him to remain at home with them. They could not bear the thought of the boy they had brought up with so much affection going so far away from them. But Veer insisted on becoming a soldier, so they let him go away, with a heavy heart and tears in their eyes.

For many days there was no news of Veer. The king went to war, vanquished his enemy and returned. The soldiers who went with him also came back home. But of Veer there was no sign. Day after day his brother and sister-in-law watched out for him, hoping to see him come walking down the road, back home. But there was no one. Then, one day, a group of soldiers passed through their village, returning

home from the war. Bhanu called out to them and asked about his brother.

'Veeru, oh yes, so sad, he died you know, in the battlefield,' said one, shaking his head.

'No no. He was injured, and he recovered. Did he not come home?' said another.

'He was on his way home when he fell ill,' informed a third.

On hearing these awful news, Bhanu was deeply saddened. He decided he could not live at home waiting for his dear little brother to return. He would go and look for him. When he told his wife, Bharati too decided to go with him. Together, they set off one day to look for the missing Veer and bring him home.

They decided to go to the site of the king's big battle, where Veer was last seen by his companions. This place was far away and they had to travel through forests and valleys and mountains and deserts. The two walked and walked, over many miles, but poor Bharati was not strong enough. One day, after travelling through a thick forest, they reached a little hamlet. Bharati sat down, exhausted. Then to Bhanu's great horror she died out of sheer exhaustion. Unable to bear his grief, Bhanu too died immediately.

Over many years at the place where the couple had died, two trees grew. One was a tall tree and the other a creeper that hugged the tree. It was as if Bharati and Bhanu were together even in death.

Meanwhile, Veer, the brother they had loved so deeply, was not really dead. He had got terribly wounded in the war and spent many years recovering from his injuries in a little village far away from home. When he finally recovered, he came back as fast as he could to his old house, knowing how anxious his family would be for him.

But imagine his surprise when he found the house locked and bolted, abandoned for many years. Slowly the neighbours gathered around and told him how Bhanu had decided to go looking for his lost brother.

That night Veer cried many bitter tears. How would he find his beloved brother and sister-in-law now? Where were they? By the time morning dawned he had made up his mind. He would try and go the way they had travelled and find them. Immediately he set off.

Veer was a soldier, but he had only lately recovered from many wounds and was not too strong. It took him many days to walk across the difficult land Bhanu and his wife had crossed. Then one day, near a forest, he came across a little shrine. The villagers told him the sad story of how the shrine came to be. Years ago a couple had arrived at the spot, tired from days of walking. Legend had it that they were on the way looking for a long-lost brother. When the

Sudha Murty

two died without fulfilling this wish, two wonderful plants, unknown to anyone earlier, had grown at the spot. The leaves and nuts from the trees were so sweet and refreshing that the villagers decided to build a small temple for the man and the woman at the place.

Veer listened to the story with growing sorrow. He realized the couple they talked about was none other than his brother and his wife. Unable to bear the news, he turned into a statue of limestone.

Do you know how they have all been remembered ever since? The tall tree grew nuts called areca nuts, the creeper's leaves were paan or betel leaves and from the statue came the lime paste that is added to preparations of paan. And this is how this loving family came together even after death. Together they taught people the values of love, unity and loyalty, and when people chew paan they remember this story about them.

—

Sharan's mom was surprised to hear this story. 'Really, Ajji,' she said, 'even I was not aware why these three ingredients are always used to make a paan. I too will come to listen to your stories from now on!'

Ajji nodded, then she added with that glint in her eyes, 'Chewing paan is not good for your teeth. Everyone, off you go to brush your teeth!'

Payasam for a Bear

Ajja and Vishnu Kaka were planning something! They could be spotted grinning and nodding and whispering. The children were dying to know what it was. Then one evening, they finally broke the news. They were all going on a picnic! It would be a picnic at the nearby falls. These waterfalls were really beautiful, with the river meandering close by and the forest just across. The children got even more excited when the two grandpas revealed the rest of the plan. Tomorrow would be a rest day for Ajji and Sharan's mother, because all the cooking would be done by them and the children! And they would do it the traditional way, by gathering firewood and then cooking the meal from scratch.

The children were so excited they could hardly sleep that night. All they could talk about was the picnic and what they would cook. Before nodding off they had decided the menu—pulao and kheer! Payasam or kheer is so easy to make, and who doesn't love it?

The next day, even the usual late risers were up and about and ready to set out for the picnic by seven o'clock. Oh, what a beautiful spot it was! They all ran around exclaiming over everything and getting ready with their cricket bats and balls for a game. Ajji sat comfortably under a big tree. Then it was time to get lunch ready. Everyone started looking for twigs to use as firewood. Ajji spotted Divya straying towards the dense thicket of trees and called out, 'Divya, come back, don't go there. Who knows what animal is there, and on top of that you all are going to cook payasam . . .'

Minu's ears pricked up immediately. 'Why Ajji, what does payasam have to do with animals?'

Ajji grinned, 'But bears love payasam! Don't you know?'

Everyone declared they had never known this piece of information. So cooking and games forgotten, young and old gathered around her to hear the story of a bear who wanted to eat payasam.

Did you know that you must never ever anger a bear? It is true; an angry bear can do some really awful things, so it is always safer to keep your word to him. Poor Mohan and Basanti did not know this, and tried to trick a bear, and see what happened to them!

Mohan had a banana plantation, where he grew delicious bananas. He also had a huge mango tree that provided him with baskets of juicy mangoes every summer. He would sell these fruits in the market and lived happily enough with his wife, Basanti.

Once, his trees yielded an exceptionally large crop of bananas and mangoes, and he decided to sell them in the market in the city, where he would get a higher price for them. So off he went with his sacks and baskets to the city. There he sat in the market, sold everything that he had brought, and made quite a bit of money. At the market, he ran into an old friend, Amar. Mohan and Amar were overjoyed to see each other after many years.

'Come to my house, dear friend,' insisted Amar. 'Let us enjoy a good meal and talk about our childhood days.'

Mohan thought this was a wonderful idea, and went with Amar to his house. There the two friends ate huge quantities of rice, dal, lovely vegetables and all kinds of sweets. Then, finally, out came the best part of the meal—the payasam!

Payasam is known by many names all over India. Some call it kheer, some payesh, and others payasam. It is made with milk, rice and jaggery and many other ingredients; and it is always yummy! So was the payasam that Amar served his friend. It was made with fragrant rice, creamy milk, sweet as sugar jaggery, and strewn with nuts, cardamoms, saffron and all kinds of wonderful, mouth-watering things. Mohan ate and ate, bowl after bowl, of this dessert till he was ready to burst.

Then the two friends chatted and rested, till it was time for Mohan to head back home. When he reached his house, he told his wife about the scrumptious meal, particularly the payasam he had eaten. Oh, how Basanti sighed and longed to have tasted this dish too! Seeing her face Mohan suggested, 'See, I have earned plenty of money by selling the fruits. Why don't I buy some of the things required to make payasam, which you can cook and both of us will enjoy it together?'

Basanti thought this was a wonderful idea. But first Mohan needed to go to the forest to collect some firewood. Then he could go to the shop and get all that was required to make the dessert. So off Mohan went, swinging his axe and whistling a tune. Now who would be sitting dozing under a tree in the forest, but a big black bear. He had just had some nice berries for lunch and was enjoying his snooze, when Mohan walked by. First the bear opened one eye, then another, and watched as Mohan cut a few branches of a nearby tree and collected twigs for firewood. Just as Mohan was tying it all up in a neat bundle, the bear spoke up.

'Hi there, friend. Where are you off to in such a happy mood, and why are you collecting so much of firewood? Tell me, are you cooking a feast tonight?'

Mohan was astonished and a little scared to be addressed like this by a bear. 'Y-yes, your honour, I mean, dear bear, ss-sir,' he mumbled and stammered.

The bear was happy after his meal, so he decided to chat some more with Mohan.

'So tell me, what are you going to cook tonight?' he asked, patting his tummy.

'P-p-payasam,' answered Mohan.

'Paya . . . what?' the bear was puzzled.

'Pa-ya-sam,' Mohan said slowly. 'It's a sweet dish.'

'Tell me more!' The bear was intrigued.

So Mohan described payasam and how it is made. As he talked about milk and rice and nuts and jaggery, the bear's eyes started gleaming, his stomach started rumbling, and he realized he absolutely, totally needed to taste this wonderful human food.

'Oh Mohan, my friend, do let me come and share your payasam tonight,' the bear begged.

Mohan was astonished. A bear as a guest for dinner! Who knows how much he would eat! But neither could he say no—that seemed so rude, and the bear was looking at him hopefully.

He sighed and replied, 'All right. You can come. But to cook so much of payasam I will need much more firewood. Can you bring that with you?'

Cunning Mohan thought he would make the bear do his work for him, so he would not need to come to the forest for the next few days.

'Yes yes!' the bear jumped up. 'Just tell me how much firewood you need. Ten? Twenty? Thirty bundles?'

'Umm, fifty would be enough,' decided Mohan. Then he slung his bundle of firewood over his shoulder and went back home. On the way he bought lots of milk, rice and everything else they would need to make the payasam.

When he reached home he told Basanti about the unusual guest who would come to share their dessert. So Basanti cooked a huge quantity of payasam. She added lovely nuts, aromatic saffron, sweet cardamoms and many wonderful things into it as she cooked. Oh, how marvellous the payasam smelt. Unable to wait any longer, the two started eating helping after helping of the dish, without waiting for their bear guest to turn up. They ate and ate and ate, till they realized they had eaten up everything! There was not a grain of rice, nor half a nut left for him!

They sat around wondering what to do. What would they say to the bear when he came expecting to eat payasam? Then, a devious plan entered Mohan's head. What if they made payasam with all kinds of other ingredients? After all, it was only a bear, and he had never tasted this dish earlier, so how would he know what it really tasted like?

The naughty man and his wife then took a little bit of milk, added lots of water to it, threw in a handful of rice, and instead of jaggery and nuts and spices they added pebbles and sand and cardamom husks and stirred and stirred the mixture till it looked somewhat like payasam. They placed the brass pot filled with this in front of the house and went and hid in the bushes somewhere at the back.

As soon as night fell, a huge dark figure appeared down the road. On its back it carried fifty bundles of firewood. It was the bear, come to dinner!

He reached Mohan's house and looked around. There was no one. Then, right in front of the house, he spotted the pot full of payasam. Unable to wait any longer, he flung down the bundles he had carried and fell upon the payasam. Only after he had eaten more than half the potful did he realize something was wrong. The milk was watery, the rice was half cooked and there was horrible grit and pebbles between his teeth! Ugh!

Oh, how angry he was now! Furious, he shouted out for Mohan. But Mohan was cowering behind the bushes and did not reply. Now angrier than ever, the bear spotted the mango tree and rubbed his

back against it. The mangoes came raining down, he shook the tree so hard. The bear continued to stamp and shake the tree, till it fell with a huge crash right on to the banana field and crushed the best banana plants. Seeing the firewood he had carried all the way from the forest lying around, the bear started throwing them around. One fell into the oven in the kitchen and set fire to the house. Soon Mohan and Basanti's house was in flames, his field in ruins and his prized mango plant destroyed.

Finally satisfied that he had taken his revenge the bear stormed back into the forest. When Mohan and his wife crawled out of their hiding place and came back home they saw everything was in ruins. How they wailed and wept and wished they hadn't been so greedy as to not leave the bear his share of payasam.

But what was the use of lamenting now? The damage was done, and the greedy couple had learnt what I told you earlier—never anger a bear! And if you make a promise to one, keep it!

Fire on the Beard

What a grand picnic everyone had! They played and ate and splashed in the water till late evening. Ajja and Ajji had to drag them back home. That night the children tumbled into bed and were fast asleep even before Ajji switched off the lights. Quietly she tucked them in. The next morning there was no sign of anyone waking up. Ajja and Ajji went about their work, not waking the children. But when it was ten o'clock, Ajji decided they had to wake up now. So she came into the room and found all four were up and chatting in bed. She looked at them for a while with her hands on the hips. Then she said, 'So, I think you've had enough rest. Now up all of you. Wash up and get ready. I'll give you your lunch by twelve noon.'

All the others jumped up except Anand. He grinned at Ajji and said, 'You know, I can live without food if I get to lie in bed all day.'

'Really?' Ajji said. 'So be it. Everyone else, lunch will be ready at twelve, so be there on time. Oh, and those who lie around in bed will also miss the afternoon story.' Then she walked off trying to hide a smile. Anand and miss a meal! He was the one who loved his food the most!

Anand was quiet. The rest sprang out of their beds and went to brush their teeth and have a bath. Soon the aroma of onion dosa wafted through the house. It was too delicious to resist. Everyone gathered in the kitchen to help grind the dosa batter.

By now Anand was bored and hungry, lying alone in bed. He quietly went and took his bath. He was worried, what if Ajji had taken him seriously and not kept a share of the dosa for him? And what if he had to miss that day's story? When Ajji saw him appear at the kitchen and join in, she laughed and said, 'You have become like Brij.'

'Who is Brij, Ajji?'

So Ajji started the story while the children ate the dosas.

Yaaawwnnn! Brij stretched out in the sun, yawned loud and long, and went back to sleep. Is Brij a rich man on a holiday; or has he worked hard all day and is just resting for a while? Neither! Brij was the laziest, most good-for-nothing fellow you'll ever meet. He would spend entire days just lying around on his bed doing nothing. He was too lazy to even trim his beard and it had grown right down to his knees. All day he sat around combing it and admiring it, doing nothing else. His mother would call him; his wife would scold him, but Brij was not one to mend his ways.

This is how most conversations with his wife, Shanti, would go:

'Can you get some water from the well? There is no water in the house.'

'The well is dry. There's no water there.'

'Can you fetch water from the pond, at least?'

'The pond is too far. I can't walk so much for a pot of water.'

'Then pluck those coconuts from the tree.'

'Oh, those coconuts are still tender. Let's pluck them next month.'

'What about getting some areca nuts from the tree then?'

'Don't you know, areca nuts are not good for health?'

'Help me plough the field then.'

'It is too hot. The sun will burn my skin. It's better if you too did not go there.'

'Can you at least look after the house when I am in the field?'

'There is nothing to look after in the house.'

And so on and on Brij would make excuses for not doing any work that was asked of him. Of course he was never too tired to eat! As soon as his wife would lay out the meal, he would jump out of bed saying, 'Oh you have prepared food for me with such love, it is my duty to eat it.' And then he would gobble down all that was given.

When evening fell, Brij would roll out of bed, comb his hair and beard and set off to meet his gang of friends. Seeing how he managed to get out of doing any work, many others in the village had decided to do the same. All these people had formed a club, The Idlers' Club. They would meet every evening and sit around and talk about all kinds of things. They claimed this way they were improving their general knowledge, but all they were really doing was gossip and boast.

Brij, as the leader of the club, would get to boast the loudest and longest. One day, the topic was who is the laziest of all.

'Bathing every day is such a waste of time and precious water. I take a bath once in two days. That way I even save water!' said Manoj, the environmentalist.

'I never make my bed,' boasted Suresh, the innkeeper. 'Why bother when you have to lie down in it once again at the end of the day?'

'I eat my food out of the vessel in which it is cooked,' claimed Raju, the cook. 'Putting the food in the plate only increases the work for you will need to wash it too.'

Now Brij thought he should say something that would beat all these other tall tales. So he said, 'I am always cool and calm. Why, even if my beard were to catch fire I would start digging a well at that time, and never store water close at hand!'

As these discussions were happening, a real fire broke out in the village! It burned down buildings and roofs and sheds, crackling and throwing up sparks; making villagers run helter-skelter looking for water to douse the flames.

The Idlers' Club heard all the commotion but no one bothered to step out to see what was happening. 'What is going on?' they only asked each other.

'Oh nothing,' Brij dismissed the topic. 'Must be some circus or the other. So, what were we talking about?'

By now the fire had spread to their road. It was fast making its way to the house where the idlers were sitting. It got hotter and hotter. Brij's friends started sweating and getting nervous now. Soon the roof of the house caught fire. Still Brij kept saying, 'Don't worry, don't worry. It will rain now and put

this out.' Then 'The wind is blowing in the opposite direction and will blow it down. We are really cool people, we should not be afraid of a fire!'

Finally his friends could stand it no longer and rushed screaming out of the house. But Brij was too stubborn, and refused to move. Finally the fire caught up with him and his beard started getting singed. Now even Brij was scared. 'Heellp!' he shouted.

'Now you can start digging the well,' his friends suggested.

'Oh, get me some water from the pond,' Brij begged.

'That's too far away,' the others shouted from outside. 'Maybe it will rain,' they added.

By now the beard was burning away merrily, and all Brij could do was leap and dance away from the flames. Till suddenly there were splashes and splashes of water! Someone was emptying cool cool water on the fire and putting it out!

Brij could not believe his luck. Who had saved him? Why, it was Shanti and many other women of the village who had worked hard and drawn water from wells and ponds to save their homes.

Finally Brij learnt his lesson. Being lazy and pretending to be cool had certainly not helped him in his hour of need. So he shaved off his half burnt beard, woke up early each morning and did all that Shanti told him to do, and more!

The Way You Look at It

On a sleepy afternoon, while the sun continued to shine, the clouds opened up and it started to rain. Sharan had fallen asleep after eating at least fifteen pooris for lunch. When he woke up, he saw a rainbow in the sky. There was a mild drizzle and the bright sunshine of summer. In the sky was a bold, bright, clear rainbow. Sharan ran to Ajji's house and started calling out to his friends.

Suma and Krishna were playing in the garden. Raghu and Divya were reading. Anand was sleeping. Sharan was so excited he called out to each one, 'Ajja, Ajji, Suma, Krishna, Raghu, Anand, Divya, come and see this!' Everyone rushed out to see what was up. The children gazed in amazement at the rainbow. Living in the city, none of them ever got to see such a vast expanse of the sky, unhindered by tall buildings. Ajja and Ajji were used to it and went back to their work.

That evening, while having their milk, the children were talking about rainbows. 'The colours of the rainbow are known as VIBGYOR,' said Raghu.

'A rainbow is called Indra Dhanush in Sanskrit,' said Suma.

'It is known as Kamanabillu in Kannada—the bow of Lord Kamadeva,' said Sharan's mother.

'In the olden days if the sun and rain came together, we used to say it is the fox's wedding and all of us have to go on the rainbow to reach the wedding,' said Ajji.

'Ultimately it is the same thing, seven colours that appear in the sky when the sun's rays are reflected by the rainwater,' said Ajja. 'It depends upon the way you look at it.'

Ajji nodded. 'The same thing appears different, depending on the way you look at it, and today I can tell you a story about that.' Immediately everyone turned their attention from the sky to Ajji.

During one monsoon season, it rained and rained in Chitpur, a little village by a mighty river. It rained so hard that the river swelled up. Huge waves lashed against the river banks and carried away trees, houses and big chunks of earth. The villagers were really scared and prayed hard for the rains to stop.

When finally the skies cleared, one by one people emerged from their homes. One of them was Raju. He walked down to the river side. There he saw something that made him rub his eyes in disbelief. Why, a huge black rock had appeared there out of nowhere! And what was more, the rock looked exactly like the head of Ganesha, the god with the elephant head. Raju immediately prostrated himself in front of the rock. 'Ganesha not only heard our prayers and made the rains go away, he has come himself to protect us!' Raju shouted to no one in particular. 'I must tell everyone about this!' he yelled and ran back to the village to tell the news.

Next came Chetan, the sculptor. He had spent so many days cooped up in his house waiting for the rains to stop. Now he was glad to be out in the open, and was thinking of his next piece of work. Suddenly he caught sight of the new rock by the river. It was just the right colour, worn smooth with age and river water. It was perfect for the scene he wanted to carve! Giving a whoop of joy he ran home to gather his carving tools.

Just as he turned the corner, a merchant came by on his horse. The animal was thirsty and he stopped there for it to have a drink of water from the river. He too spotted the stone. 'What a big stone!' he remarked. 'And it is nice and smooth and flat. Let me sit for a while on it and rest.' After enjoying a nice rest on the rock, the merchant decided he would tell his friends about it. They were travelling together and all of them would be thrilled to be able to sit there for some time, by the river.

He went off to find his friends.

Just then, Ajit, a soldier, came on his horse. He got down and washed his face. While his horse was drinking water, he was looking around and the same stone caught his attention. He was surprised and said to himself, 'What a huge stone on the river bed! Maybe I should get it removed so that in an emergency it should not become a hindrance on the road. Our army can march better if such obstacles are not there. I must inform my commander.' Thinking so, he rushed back to his camp to talk to his commander.

Later in the day Bholu, the village washerman, appeared by the river with his big bundle of clothes. To his astonishment he found a crowd right around his favourite washing spot. They were all arguing over a rock! Pushing his way into the crowd, Bholu spoke in a loud voice, 'Hey! What do you think you all are doing?'

Raju now burst out, 'This rock is a sign from Lord Ganesha, I want to worship it.'

Chetan raised his voice even louder and said, 'No no, this rock is going to be used for my next sculpture.'

The merchant shouted, 'I have invited all my friends to rest on it! It is ours!'

Ajit was giving orders to remove the stone to his soldiers.

Bholu now grinned and said, 'But this rock has been here for years and years! Earlier half of it was submerged in the mud. Now with the rains the mud has got washed off, and you are seeing more of it. The washermen of Chitpur have been using this rock to do our washing for many, many years! There's nothing miraculous about it. Now off with all of you, I have work to do.'

So saying Bholu emptied his bundle of clothes and set to work. What could the others do? They had to go away grumbling quietly to themselves.

Roopa's Great Escape

Ajja's and Vishnu Kaka's houses were teeming with people! There was a village festival, and friends and relatives from near and far had come to Shiggaon. There were people the children had not seen or even heard about before. Some said, 'I am your father's fourth cousin.' Someone else said, 'I am your grandmother's second cousin.' The houses were full and there was a lot of fun and laughter everywhere. Nobody expected a separate bedroom or a special dish at the dining table. They all ate together and talked to everybody and slept on the floor on mattresses. The city children were surprised at the ease with which the guests made themselves at home. The women helped out in the kitchen in the morning and in the evening they dressed in shining silk sarees and went to the fair. In fact everyone dressed in their best, put the two hundred rupees Ajja gave in their pockets and purses and made for the fair.

The fair itself was quite astonishing. The children from Mumbai said, 'It is just like Chowpati on Juhu beach.' The Delhi kids said, 'It is similar to Janpath.' Others said, 'It is like Karaga or Kallekai Parishe in Bangalore.' Vishnu Kaka explained, 'In every village there is a village god or goddess and once a year we worship them in a grand way. At the festival and fair it is not just about selling and buying, it is also about meeting people, exchanging gifts, having a feast and a good time.'

The group moved from shop to shop, peeping into the photo studios, examining bangles, waiting for a turn on the merry-go-round and clapping along to the dances, when someone noticed Suma was missing! Somewhere in the crowd she had got separated from the rest, and now there was no sign of her. Immediately her mother started wailing, and Ajji consoled her. Vishnu Kaka too looked really worried. The children were scared and thrilled too. This was just like *Home Alone*! As Vishnu Kaka was about to make his way to the police assistance booth, they heard Suma's voice on the mike! 'I am in the police station, Vishnu Ajja please come and fetch me.' When Suma was traced, her mother started scolding her. But Suma was not bothered. 'I was not worried,' she said. 'In the crowd when I realized I was not with you people, I straightaway went to the police station and told them to make an announcement.'

Everyone declared she was a very brave and sensible girl, and for a change that day Vishnu Kaka said, 'Today I will tell a story about a young girl like Suma who had a lot of courage. I read this story in a book when I was young.'

———

Once, there lived a very clever young girl called Roopa. She was an orphan and had been taken care of all her life by the people of the village in which she lived. She was very hard-working and once she became old enough, she lived all by herself and looked after herself. But she always missed having a family of her own, even though her neighbours were such loving and caring people.

One day, when Roopa was about sixteen years old, she went down to the river along with some other women and girls to wash clothes and fetch water. Diwali was around the corner and everyone was excited. They were discussing what new clothes they would get. Some were expecting their husbands and fathers to return to the village with lovely gifts for them and were looking forward to all the merrymaking that would happen over the next few days.

Only Roopa was quiet. She did not have anyone to buy her new clothes or shoes or presents. The villagers were kind to her, but they had barely enough for their own needs so how could she expect them to get anything for her? Yet today, hearing all the happy chatter around her, she could not keep quiet any longer.

'Even I will get a new sari this year!' she told Rama, her best friend.

Rama and all the other girls were astonished. Who was going to get Roopa her new sari? 'I heard from a distant uncle the other day. He was working for many years in a faraway city and did not know that my parents had died. Now that he is back, he has promised to visit me on Diwali. I am sure he will bring some marvellous gift for me!' Roopa had started weaving a story, and now she kept adding, telling all kinds of tales about her imaginary uncle. Her friends listened open-mouthed. Then they went home, telling each other what luck Roopa was finally no longer all alone in the world.

As soon as the bunch of women had gone away, who emerged from behind a tree, but Bholu the trickster. He had been sitting under the tree, planning his next theft, when he had fallen asleep. Then he had woken up and seen the women at the river and had sat there still hoping to hear something about the villagers. Sure enough, he had heard Roopa's story, and was now ready with a plan!

Bholu decided to dress up as an old man and appear at Roopa's house a few days before Diwali pretending to be her uncle! Then he would take her away along with any valuables she may have got from her parents.

A week before Diwali, an old stranger appeared at Roopa's door. He was carrying new clothes, sweets and other gifts. Roopa was out doing some errands so her neighbours came around to find out who he was. Bholu acted perfectly like Roopa's long-lost uncle, eagerly waiting to meet her. When Roopa returned home she found everyone sitting around an old man, who said he was the uncle she had made up a story about!

Roopa was astonished. How had this happened? She had only been pretending to have a relative just so her friends would not feel sorry for her, and now here he was, a real person! Then her neighbour, who had looked after her all these years, said, 'Roopa, this is your Uncle Bholu; he learnt he had a niece and came here looking for you. He wants to take you home with him and look after you like his own daughter. You are so lucky, Roopa, and we are so happy for you!'

Roopa looked around at everyone, beaming happily at her, and thought what harm would there be if she went away with this uncle. She happily packed whatever little things she owned and waving goodbye to her friends and neighbours, went off with Bholu.

No sooner had they reached his house than he took off his disguise and appeared before her as a young man. Roopa was horrified. Oh, what a fool she had been to believe his story and come away with him! He was nothing but a trickster.

In Bholu's house there was no one else but his mother, who was old and deaf and blind. After eating his lunch, Bholu decided to walk about for a while, meeting his friends and telling them how he had kidnapped Roopa. She too ate her lunch, pretended she was very sleepy, yawned loudly and told his mother, 'Aunty, I am very tired after that long journey. I am going to bed for a little while. If your son comes round tell him not to wake me up.'

Bholu's mother nodded, though she had not heard much. Roopa quickly went to the other room, borrowed some of Bholu's clothes, wore them and ran off. She took with her a few coins and a thick stick to defend herself if need be. Before leaving she arranged the pillows in such a way on the bed that in the evening darkness it looked like someone was sleeping on the bed. Then she covered the pillows with a dupatta and a sheet. If anyone only looked in from the door it would seem as if a woman was sleeping on the bed.

Bholu returned home when it was well past evening. His mother told him Roopa was in her room. He peeped in, saw someone sleeping and went away. Many hours passed, Bholu kept checking whether Roopa was awake or not, but each time he saw her sleeping without moving a muscle. Finally, he realized something was wrong.

He went up to the bed now and pulled back the dupatta and the sheet. Imagine his shock when he saw nothing but pillows on the bed! Roopa had disappeared! He ran out immediately and asked everyone around if they had seen a young, pretty girl walk out of his house. But no one had, because Roopa had cleverly disguised herself as a man!

Meanwhile, Roopa too had walked many miles till she reached a different town. There she looked around for work, and was taken in by an innkeeper to look after the guests and to show them their rooms. Roopa, who now called herself Rupesh, was happy doing this work. She could not return to her village till she did something about Bholu, otherwise he would be sure to land up there and bring her back with him, pretending to be her uncle.

After many days, Bholu turned up at the town. He walked from shop to inn to market, asking if anyone had seen someone like Roopa. Of course no one had. Roopa got to know and decided to teach him a lesson. When Bholu reached her inn, he did not recognize her in men's clothes. She agreed to give him a room for the night. She told him, 'Sir, I will give you a room in the attic. It is nice and warm and cosy there, and you will be away from this harsh winter cold.'

Bholu happily agreed and followed her to the room. A ladder was kept in the middle of the room which went up to a little trapdoor. If you climbed through the door, you entered the attic. Bholu quickly went up the ladder, found his bed, wrapped his blanket around himself and went off to sleep.

When it was the middle of the night, Roopa sneaked into the room and removed the ladder. Then she threw some marbles right under the trapdoor and stamped loudly around the room. Bholu woke with a start. Who was that walking around his room? He called down nervously, 'W-who is there?'

Roopa called out in her man's voice, 'Nothing to worry sir. The soldiers are looking for a thief they believe is hiding in this inn.'

Bholu was really scared. How did the soldiers know he was a thief and a trickster? He was sure they were looking for him, and decided to make a run for it. He opened the trapdoor and stepped down. But there was no ladder! Bholu fell with a loud thud on to the floor! When he tried to get up, his feet slipped on the many marbles strewn about the room and he went crashing and sliding all over the place! Finally he hit his head against a wall and passed out, unconscious.

Roopa had been watching this from the door with great delight. Her plan was working! As soon as Bholu fainted, she heaved him up and packed him up into a large box. She placed a nice silk cloth on top of him. Then she dragged the box outside the inn and stood there.

Soon a bullock cart passed by with two travellers heading for the inn. When they saw Roopa, or Rupesh, stand outside the inn, they asked, 'Are you the manager of this inn?'

Roopa nodded yes.

'Why are you standing here then?'

Roopa replied in a worried voice, 'I look after this inn. I was supposed to go to my own village earlier today to attend a wedding. But there was so much of work that I could not leave, and now here I am waiting for my cart with this heavy box.' Then she lowered her voice and whispered, 'This box is full of gifts I bought for the wedding, and if I don't reach in time everyone will be really disappointed.'

The two travellers, who were up to no good themselves, looked at each other. The same thought had come to both! They said, 'Don't worry, brother. You can take a ride on our cart. Why don't you put your box on the cart here? But before we start, would you mind getting us a drink of water?'

Rupesh, or Roopa, smiled to herself, and dragged the box on to the cart. Then she went inside to fetch the water. She took her time. As soon as her back was turned, the two travellers opened the box to see what it contained. They saw some lovely silk cloth on top. Now assured that they had got their hands on some valuables, they quickly urged their bullocks forward and made a dash for it. Once they were well and truly out of sight, Roopa grinned to herself. Her plan had worked! She ran to the nearest police station, and told them all about the theft.

The two men in the bullock cart were just celebrating their theft of the box, when they were horrified to see soldiers waiting for them down the road. What could they do, they wondered. They were crossing a bridge over a river at that time, and quickly tipped the box into the water. Then they heaved a sigh of relief and went their way.

So that was the end of Bholu, and Roopa too returned to her village, where she lived happily on her own. She was not going to trust any stranger any more!

'And that's what brave Suma did too! When she was in trouble she did not talk to any stranger, but went straight to the police for help. We must always remain cool like this when in trouble,' signed off Vishnu Kaka. Suma was delighted at this praise, and ate her bhajias with great happiness all the way home!

Five Spoons of Salt

One morning, Ajji told Ajja, 'Today is a Santhe (a village market day which happens once in a week). Why don't you take the children and show them the Santhe and buy vegetables and other things for the house?' Ajja, who normally would have said yes, was hesitant. 'How will I manage all the children, that too at the Santhe? Remember what happened at the jatre—the fair? At least there they had a temporary police assistance booth. There will be nothing of the sort at the Santhe.' Ajji agreed. This was a problem. Then she had an idea. 'Why don't we ask Vishnu if he can spare Damu for a few hours? Damu can accompany you and help see that the children are all right.'

Damu was Vishnu Kaka's right-hand man. Everyone called him 'Mr Dependable'. He drove the car, cooked, looked after the fields, the accounts and made sure Vishnu Kaka was well cared for. Without him Vishnu Kaka could not run the house or do anything in the fields. Vishnu Kaka's son lived with his family in Delhi and came only for holidays, so Damu was his real companion.

So it was that all seven children and Damu and Ajja were now ready to visit the Santhe. Damu had a plan. 'The Santhe is only two kilometres away. Why don't we walk, and let your Ajja go in the auto?' The children were horrified. Walk for two kilometres in the heat! 'It would be so boring too!' added Raghu. But Damu had made up his mind. 'Walk with me. I will tell you such wonderful stories that you will forget everything, even the heat!'

The children agreed. Then Meenu had a condition. 'It has to be a true story, Damu Anna!'

Damu was unfazed. 'I'll tell you a story about my sister. Do you know how I came to be "Mr Dependable"? I saw what happened to her once because she was forgetful and decided never to let that happen to me.'

So he started his story.

'Gita, where are you? I need you to run down to the store and get these medicines for me!' Gita's grandfather called out for her. Where was Gita? She was lying in bed, reading a book! For a long time she pretended not to have heard what her grandfather was saying. The book was just too exciting, and it was so hot outside, she really did not feel like stirring out of bed.

'Gita!' This time her mother's voice also called out to her. With a sigh the girl got out of bed and went to see what needed to be done. Her grandfather handed her some money and said, 'I have a really bad headache since morning. Will you get these medicines for me?'

Gita took the money and set off for the store. On the way she passed by a sweet shop. Oh, what lovely gulab jamoons and laddoos and jalebis were displayed! She had to have some. Forgetting all about her errand she entered the shop and started tucking into sweets. Soon a friend came by and joined her. The two girls ate and chatted for a really long time. Gita had forgotten all about her poor grandfather with his headache! Afternoon turned to evening, the medicine store shut for the day, when Gita remembered why she had stepped out of her house. When she hurried back home, how upset her grandfather was. 'When will you grow up, Gita, and become responsible?' he sighed and asked.

Gita felt really bad, but did she mend her ways? No, she remained the same forgetful person. When her mother told her to collect the clothes from the washing line outside, she remembered to do so only the next morning! By then the clothes were soaked through all over again because of the overnight rains. Another day, she had to take her sister's lunch box to the school. On the way she saw a circus was in town. All morning Gita spent wandering around the circus tents, watching the animals eating and training for their acts. It was only when she felt hungry herself did she look down at the lunch box in her hand and realized her sister must have gone home by then, after spending a day in school without her lunch.

Another time her father, while rushing to get ready for work, asked if she could quickly iron his shirt. Gita picked up the shirt and placed it on the ironing table next to the window. Just then the fruit vendor passed by with big, fat, juicy mangoes in his basket! Of course Gita forgot all about the hot iron sitting on the shirt and got engrossed in choosing the best mangoes to buy. Only when smoke started billowing out and the shirt had burnt as crisp as a toast did she look around and see what had happened. Her father was very upset indeed that day.

Some days after this incident, Gita came home from school and announced that the whole class was being taken for a picnic the next day. The teacher had asked each student to bring one food item from home which would be shared by all the children. Gita had chosen to bring sambar. She was very proud of her mother's tasty, tangy sambar and was eager to share it with her friends so they could taste it too. Gita's mother agreed to make a big pot of sambar for her to take to the picnic the next day, and that night Gita went to bed feeling very happy, dreaming about the exciting day ahead.

The next morning her mother woke up early and started making the sambar. She boiled the dal, added the vegetables, coconut and all the spices, and set the pot boiling on the stove. Soon a delicious aroma wafted out from the pot and tickled Gita's nose as she lay sleeping in bed. Seeing her stir, her mother told her, 'Gita wake up now, dear. See the sambar is nearly done. I am going to the temple, so after some time just add five teaspoons of salt to it. Don't forget now, and wake up and get ready quickly!'

So saying she bustled off. Gita's grandmother, who was in the kitchen, heard all this and muttered to herself, 'When will my daughter-in-law learn that Gita can never remember anything. I'm sure the girl will forget to add the salt. Then she will be teased by all her friends. Better be careful.' So saying she went and added the salt in the pot.

Gita's grandfather was sitting on the veranda reading his newspaper. He remembered only too well the day he had spent with a headache waiting for Gita to return with the medicines which never came. 'Gita and remember something? That'll be the day!' he muttered, and went into the kitchen and added the salt in the sambar himself.

Gita's sister was combing her hair, ready to go off to school. She too recalled the day she had spent feeling hungry in school waiting for Gita to turn up with her lunch box. Sure that Gita would forget about the salt and be laughed at by her friends, she quickly went into the kitchen and added five spoons of salt.

Gita's brother was brushing his teeth and hearing his mother's words to his sister, guessed she would forget about the salt. He dropped in a few spoons of salt into the pot and went off.

Gita's father was carefully ironing his own shirt. Like the others he too slipped into the kitchen and added salt to the pot of sambar.

By now Gita had woken up and wonder of wonders, remembered she needed to add the salt! So she too went and added five teaspoons as her mother had told her to do. By now her mother had returned and quickly poured the sambar into a big container and sent her daughter off for her picnic.

At the picnic spot the children had a wonderful time, roaming around and playing. Soon they were too hungry to do anything else. Out came the plates and spoons and all the containers filled to the brim with food. Plates were piled up with rice, chutneys, vegetables, pooris and all kinds of goodies. Everyone took large helpings of the sambar as Gita served it out. But no sooner than they put the first spoonful in their mouths, 'Blaagh! Horrible! Water!' everybody started shouting. Astonished, Gita wondered what was wrong, then gingerly tasted the rice and sambar on her own plate. It was disgusting! It was as if her mother had dredged out all the salt in the sea and added it to the sambar! Then Gita remembered, her mother had not added the salt, she had! So what had gone wrong?

That day everyone in Gita's house waited eagerly for her to get back from school and tell them about her wonderful outing. But what was this? She came

trudging back, her face sad and tear-stained. What had happened? Gita burst out at them, 'Did anyone else add salt in the sambar?'

'I did!' said her grandmother.

'I did too!' said Grandfather.

'So did I!' said Father.

'Me too!' said her brother.

'And I!' said her sister.

They all looked at each other in dismay. No wonder Gita looked so sad. Her friends would have made her feel miserable about the salty sambar!

'Why did you all do it? Amma had told only me to do so!' Gita wept.

'Oh dear, you forget everything you are told to do, so we thought . . . perhaps . . . you wouldn't remember this time too,' all of them said sadly.

Now her mother pulled her close, wiped away her tears and said, 'See, all this happened because no one could believe you could do anything without being reminded many times about it. Promise you will be a careful, responsible girl from now on, and we will all trust you to do your work.'

Gita sniffed and nodded her head. She did become much more careful with her chores after that. And it took a lot of convincing, but her friends did come to her house for lunch one day to taste her mother's delicious cooking, especially her tasty tangy sambar, and everyone agreed it was the best sambar they had ever eaten!

When the story was over, the children realized they were already at the Santhe. There were heaps of vegetables, sweets, flowers all around. There were goats, cows, buffaloes, fish, chicken and eggs for sale. The smell of nuts, cardamom and other spices hung in the air. It was unlike the fair where people had come to have a good time. Here a lot of business was taking place and everyone was buying and selling busily. The fruits and vegetables were very fresh.

The flowers looked as if they had just been plucked. Everyone was friendly.

The fruit vendor saw Ajja and said, 'Namaste Masterji. Oh! You have come with your grandchildren. It is nice to see everyone like this.' Then he gave each one a mango. When Ajja offered money, he wouldn't take it. He said, 'After all you were my masterji, my teacher. Can't I give seven mangoes as gifts to your grandchildren? They are from my garden, not that I purchased them.' The children were delighted at his warmth and kindness and returned home very happy that day.

How the Seasons Got their Share

It was an unusually hot afternoon, and there was a power cut. The children were sitting in the house, wiping their foreheads and complaining. 'How do you stay without electricity, Ajja?' asked Raghu. 'In Mumbai, in our apartment, if ever the electricity goes off, the generator comes on automatically. We never even know that the power has gone.' Ajja looked around at the hot sweaty faces, and said, 'All right, I'll show you a place which is as cool as an AC room. And it stays that way without any electricity! Come on everyone, grab a mat each and follow me.'

The children were intrigued. Ajja walked out into the garden, crossed it, right till the old neem tree that stood in a corner. Ajja told them to spread their mats under the tree and lie down. It was deliciously cool and comfortable under the tree. Everyone lay down and looked up at the gently moving leaves on the great branches over their heads. This was so much more fun than lying in a closed room! Ajja too had pulled up a comfortable old easy chair and was nodding off. After some time he said, 'This is why I love summer! What seasons do you children prefer?'

Immediately Anand said, 'I too like summer, because there is no school, and we can eat ice cream and mangoes. We can also go swimming.'

'I don't like summer, I like winter. You can wear colourful sweaters and eat different kinds of fruits. It is nice and cosy to be at home. You can drink hot soup and hot chocolate,' said Krishna.

'I don't like winter, I get an ear pain. I prefer the rainy season. It is so nice when it rains and all the trees look so fresh and happy,' said Meenu.

'What about you, Raghu? Why are you silent?' Ajja asked.

'I like all the seasons, provided someone like you or Ajji is there with us.'

Ajja smiled. 'Well, each season has its own beauty and use. We could not do without even one.'

'How is that?' asked the children.

'Okay, I will tell you a story about what happened once when the seasons starting fighting with one another.'

God stepped back and looked happily at the Earth he had just created. He had filled it with humans, animals, trees and seas and it looked a wonderful place to be in. But something was missing. After thinking for a while, he called out to six brothers: Day, Night, Summer, Winter, Monsoon and Wind. He commanded the six brothers to go down to Earth and help the creatures there live comfortably and prosper. 'You must help the creatures on Earth grow food and live comfortably. I have divided Time into two parts—twenty-four hours and 365 days. You must share this among yourselves so that people on Earth get all that they need.' The six brothers nodded obediently, but no sooner was God's back turned than they all started quarrelling!

Everyone wanted a big share of the time available to spend on Earth. Day and Night decided each would get twenty-four hours each. But the seasons kept quarrelling. Summer was the eldest, so he said, 'I will be on Earth for 365 days first!'

Rain said, 'If I don't show up all the water on Earth will disappear, so I will come next.'

Winter said, 'After the rains I help trees to flower, so I will come in the third year.'

Poor Wind was the youngest and no one paid him any attention, so he got the last year.

So life started on Earth. For twenty-four hours at a

time there was Day, then twenty-four hours of Night. Summer continued for one whole year. While in the beginning the heat helped the crops to grow, soon it became too hot for anyone to do anything. All the water dried up and there was great discomfort. The people of Earth pleaded with Summer to stop and he had to leave before his year was up.

Then it was the turn of Rain. When he started pouring down, how happy everyone was to get some respite from the year's summer. But soon the lakes, ponds, rivers, oceans all filled to the brim and started overflowing. The crops got spoilt in the rain and there was nothing for anyone to eat. When people prayed for him to stop, he had to step aside and make way for Winter.

With relief people greeted Winter. Now there was neither the scorching sun nor the pouring rain. But when day after day went by like this they started falling sick from the constant cold, the plants started dying because of less sunshine. At the people's request Winter too had to stop.

Now it was the turn of Wind. Within a few days of his constant huffing and puffing people were scared to step out anywhere. Trees were uprooted, the roofs of houses went flying and there was chaos all around.

The brothers realized what they had done would displease God mightily. So they decided to change their ways. Instead of each taking a year they decide

to share one year among each other. But again, Wind being the youngest got left out and got no time for himself. He sat in a corner and sulked.

During summer time people sowed their crops and waited for the rains. Rain came with loads of water but there was no wind to distribute it equally. Some parts of Earth got buckets of rain and other parts none at all. Now everyone realized that Wind was as important. They called out to him and he finally agreed to do his work. But he did not get a separate time for himself. He was allowed to blow all through the year. So in Summer he blew and helped reduce the heat. During rains he blew the clouds from one place to another and took rainwater everywhere. In Winter he still blew and made it even colder!

Day and Night too learnt from the four brothers and decided to divide the twenty-four hours equally. So one half was Day and the other was Night.

Now everyone on Earth was happy, and the six brothers learnt to share their time.

By this time Ajji called from the house, 'The electricity is back. You can come inside now.' But the children were happy to remain outside and enjoy the breeze.

The Island of Statues

One day, early in the morning, the children heard a loud voice booming outside. 'Where are your grandchildren? I have come to take them to my place.' They went running out to see a very tall man with twinkling eyes and a grey beard sipping coffee with their grandparents. He wore a crisp white dhoti and shirt and a black cap. His smile was so charming that the children instantly warmed to him. Ajji was shaking her head and saying, 'Rehmat, there's no way Peerambhi can manage four children. Take them out for the day, why do you want to have them over for the night?' But the man called Rehmat shook his head. 'No no, I will take them for a night's stay. My Usman is a great cook and will look after everything. Peerambhi will not be troubled at all.'

Ajji saw the questioning look on the children's faces and explained, 'This is Rehmat. A long time back when your Ajja was a schoolteacher, he was your Ajja's student. He lives a little far away now. He has a mango grove there, and a large house. All his children live abroad. In his house there's a large library of books and what can be called a mini zoo with goats, cows, peacocks, pigeons and parrots. He wants to have you all over for the night. I'm sure you'll have a good time, but do you want to go?'

'He also tells very beautiful stories,' added Ajja.

Rehmat grinned and said, 'Masterji, don't exaggerate. I started reading children's story books only after my grandchildren were born. Then I remembered the stories you used to tell us in school and passed off some of them as my own.' He turned to the children and said, 'So what do you think, kids, will you come with me? I will show you a different part of the village.'

Everyone was thinking, when Raghu spoke up, 'Can we bring our friends with us?'

'Oh, you mean Vishnu Kaka's grandchildren? Of course they can come. The more the merrier. Peerambhi will love having so many children in the house.'

Raghu ran to Sharan's house to give the news.

Rehmat Chacha, as everyone called him, had brought a jeep and soon all seven had packed a change and their toothbrushes and piled into it. Rehmat Chacha's house was far, about thirty kilometres away, and on the way they had to go through a forest. The road cutting through the forest was narrow and winding. Tall trees stood on both sides. It was a dark, scary place. Suma looked around nervously and said, 'Will anyone ever cut down these trees and widen the road?'

Rehamt Chacha shook his head. 'Oh no, the villagers will never allow it. We love our trees and try to see as few are cut down as possible. Trees must never be cut unnecessarily. Do you want to listen to a story about a kingdom that cut down all its trees?'

Of course the children did, so Rehmat Chacha began his story.

Once there was a beautiful verdant green island. It had forests filled with huge trees, waterfalls gushing with clear blue water and mountains where there was a quarry of a unique kind of stone. This stone was valued for its attractive white colour. It was also easy to turn into sculptures.

The island had been ruled for years by a king who was now old. He looked after his people well and loved the natural beauty of his land above all. His closest friend was a sculptor called Amar. Amar too loved the land more than anything else. He had a

school where students from far and wide came to learn the art of creating sculptures out of stone. But Amar had one odd condition for the students who studied in his school. He insisted they bring their own supply of stone! Only for their final sculpture were they allowed to use a piece of stone from the island's quarry. Many grumbled at this rule. After all, dragging tons of stone to an island in the middle of a sea was difficult, but Amar was adamant.

Once, his king asked him the reason for this condition, and this is what wise old Amar had to say: 'This stone and indeed everything on this remarkable land of ours is a gift which we need to preserve. Unless we use it wisely how will we be able to save this quarry for our children? If we start using the stones and woods from trees without a thought they will soon finish and then we will be left with an empty, barren land. This is why I insist that students learning the craft of sculpting bring their own material, and only when they make their final piece of art can they use this unique stone from our land.'

The king applauded this thought in his mind and let Amar run his school the way he wanted. But then a day came when the king, now very old, died, and his son took over the throne. Rajdip, the new king, wanted to do everything differently from his father. He started changing many laws. One day he remembered the art school and went to visit it. There he saw the students working on their sculptures. But his ministers whispered to him the complaints that other students, who had not wanted to bring their own material, had made about Amar's rule.

Rajdip realized that if he lifted the rule then many more people would come to study in the school. Their fees would add to the prosperity of the island and in addition they would create lovely works of art that could be used to beautify the towns. He ordered Amar to step down as the teacher and brought someone else to run the school.

Soon the island was full of students chipping away on the stone. Their demands increased the mining at the quarry. They created large sculptures which now needed to get transported back to the town. Trees were cut down to make carts and to clear roads. Without trees to provide wood for their boats the fishermen of the island could not go out to sea. They started fishing near the land and got into fights frequently with one another. New houses were not strong as both wood and stone were scarce. It was difficult for farmers to make good ploughs and farming suffered. All the mining created so much of pollution that plants started dying out, diseases spread, and the tinkling waterfalls fell silent as water became scarce. The climate changed, it became hotter and drier. Soon there were famines and the once beautiful green island was reduced to a wasteland of weeds and scrub.

Rajdip's wishes of lining his capital city and palace with giant sculptures was fulfilled. Each student in the art school made a beautiful huge statue and gifted it to him. Soon these statues filled up the entire kingdom. Where once there were deep forests and blue rivers and streams, the island was a barren land now. The forests were gone. The rivers had turned into dirty trickles of water. The climate had become hot and dusty as the rains no longer came on time. People started leaving the island. The houses, schools and palaces slowly fell silent as they were abandoned. With time, everyone forgot about this island. Many many years later when explorers landed here, they found hundreds of statues strewn all over a bare island: a land destroyed by the king's greed.

How everyone enjoyed the story. The rest of the journey was spent in each one acting out a part from the story, with Rehmat Chacha taking on the role of the wise old king. Cheerful and at the same time very hungry, they soon reached their new friend's house.

It was a huge rambling place. Peerambhi was waiting for them at the doorstep. She told Usman to make a sherbet of mango, and Shurukumbha (a kind of kheer) for lunch. There was also paratha, biriyani, and all kinds of mouth-watering dishes which Usman was more than happy to prepare. After lunch they roamed around the house, examined the books in the library and the many awards Rehmat Chacha had received for his innovative skills in agriculture.

The Kingdom of Fools

'Rehmat Chacha, you must be very intelligent. You know so much about farming, fishing, stories and so many other things,' Meenu remarked that night as they sat outside, watching the fireflies twinkling all around them.

But Rehmat Chacha did not agree. 'No, not really. There is plenty I still don't know. In fact, one can never stop learning. Knowledge is the only thing it's good to be greedy about.'

It was a beautiful, clear night. The moon and stars shone in the black, unpolluted sky. Peerambhi was feeling very happy. Her own grandchildren lived so far away, and came to visit her only once in two or three years. After so long the house was filled with laughter and young voices. She was too frail to do much, and was enjoying sitting among them and talking to them.

Soon they started yawning and rubbing their eyes. But no one was going to bed till Rehmat Chacha told another story!

———

There once lived a king who was very intelligent. He looked down upon anyone he thought was dull. He was also very proud about the fact that in his kingdom there were no stupid people.

Some distance away from the capital city lived an old teacher. He had taught the young prince, who was a sweet-natured boy once but had turned into a proud, rude king. Many people told him about the king's boastful nature, and the teacher decided to teach his old pupil a lesson he would never forget. He called his three best and brightest students, Harish, Mahesh and Umesh, and said, 'We need to bring that proud king down a peg or two. I want the three of you to teach him a lesson and make him realize the foolishness of his pride.'

The three students set off for the capital. Harish walked to the city market. There he met a man selling betel leaves.

'How much for these leaves?' he asked.

'Ten rupees for two hundred leaves,' the shopkeeper replied.

'Here are ten rupees. Give me only twenty-five leaves. My servant will come and collect the balance one hundred and seventy-five leaves.'

The betel-leaf seller agreed and gave Harish twenty-five leaves.

Harish now strolled into another shop where beautiful shawls were being sold.

'How much for this?' he asked, fingering the best shawl in the shop.

'Two hundred rupees,' answered the shopkeeper.

'Here are twenty-five rupees. You can collect the remaining hundred and seventy-five rupees from the paan shop there,' Harish said, handing the shopkeeper a note.

'Please give the person who brings this note the remaining one hundred and seventy-five,' the note read. The shawl shop owner sent his servant with the note to the paan shop to verify if indeed this was true. The other shopkeeper glanced at the note and said, 'Yes, it's true. I have to give him one hundred and seventy-five more. Come back in half an hour—I will count and keep them ready.'

The servant returned and whispered to his master: indeed, the betel-leaf seller was going to give them the remaining one hundred and seventy-five. Harish walked out with the shawl. After half an hour, when the servant went to collect the money, he found the shopkeeper busy counting out leaves. 'Hundred seventy-three, hundred seventy-four, hundred seventy-five . . . There you go, here are the rest of the leaves.'

The servant was amazed at being handed a sheaf of paan leaves instead of money. He called his master and the two shopkeepers started arguing loudly. Slowly they realized that someone had made fools of them. They rushed to complain to the king.

The king was surprised to hear how a stranger had tricked the clever shopkeepers of his kingdom. He decided to keep a lookout for this man.

The next day, Mahesh walked into the royal carpenter's shop. It was the middle of the afternoon

and the carpenter was in his shop tinkering with some strange looking instruments. Mahesh was well dressed, so the carpenter thought he was rich. Enthusiastically he started showing off his various creations. He picked up a large wooden lock and said, 'See this? Will you believe that with this you can even lock a man? Place the person's head between the lock and a pillar and turn the key, and there, the man cannot escape.'

Mahesh pretended to be sceptical. 'Go on now. How can a simple wooden lock do such a thing? I don't believe you.' The carpenter got very agitated. 'But it's true, sir. I am the king's carpenter after all. I create many complicated instruments for the state. Here, let me show you.' Saying this, he put the lock around his neck and the nearest pillar and turned the key. 'Now, see? I cannot even move my neck! Are you convinced? Now just turn the key the other way to set me free.'

But Mahesh would not turn the key. He just stood there laughing. Then he coolly picked up the key and walked out of the shop. The carpenter could only shout at Mahesh's retreating back. 'You villain! Come back! Set me free!' But it was in vain. Mahesh had fooled him.

Later that evening the king came to know of this other stranger who had duped his clever carpenter. He was worried. Who were these men, making the

brightest people of his kingdom look stupid? He decided to go around the city in disguise to try and catch them.

As he walked near the city gates, he found a man sitting there with a heap of mangoes, waiting for someone to buy them. The fruit seller had chosen the loneliest spot, so the king was suspicious.

'Why are you selling your fruits here?' he asked.

The fruit seller was actually Umesh. He pretended to look nervously around and answered in a whisper, 'Sir, I have heard there are some clever cheats roaming around the kingdom wanting to cheat us and our clever king. I have heard one will be walking by this way soon, so I am waiting here hoping to catch him and deliver him to the king.'

The king was surprised that this person knew all about the clever gang of cheats.

'Have you seen him before?'

'Yes, sir. I know the gang. The person who is coming today is the chief.'

'What does he look like?'

'He is tall, hefty and very cruel.'

'Is there any way I can see him?' the king asked excitedly.

'Sir, the best way is to hide. As soon as he comes, I will whistle, and you can see him.'

But at that spot there was neither a tree nor any rock behind which the king could hide. Then the fruit seller held out a sack. 'Hide in this, sir,' he suggested. 'I will keep you next to me, and anyone will think it is a sack of mangoes.'

The king agreed and hopped into the sack. Quickly Umesh tied it and walked away, laughing. The king soon realized he had been tricked. But he was tied in the sack and could do nothing. Many hours later, when his soldiers came looking for him, he managed to wriggle around in the sack and attract their attention. How embarrassed he was, to be set free by them! He also knew now that he and the people of his kingdom were not as clever as he loved to boast. He realized his mistake.

The king's old teacher came to the court and explained how his three students had tricked everyone. Harish, Mahesh and Umesh apologized for their actions. And the king promised to rule his kingdom with wisdom and humility.

The Story of Silk

No sooner had the children gotten over their excitement of the visit to Rehmat Chacha's house than Ajji sprung another surprise. There was a wedding in the village! Having attended some village weddings earlier, the children knew what to expect. Here, it was not like the city where you went at a certain time printed on the card, ate, gave your present and came back. In the village everyone was invited, whether your name was on a card or not. And not only were you expected to come as early as possible, you were also expected to pitch in and help the host! So Damu was seen rushing off in the jeep to pick up guests from the railway station. Rehmat Chacha was in charge of providing fresh vegetables from his farm. Ajji was herding a group of women

146

into the kitchen and telling them what to do. Ajja was supervising the cleanliness and had stocked up on big bottles of phenyl and other cleansers. And Vishnu Kaka was dressed in his best, most spotless dhoti and kurta and was looking after the guests.

Ajji told the children to wear their nicest clothes and come to the venue. Krishna, always careful of the way she looked, wore her pretty blue silk frock. Ajji noticed and said, 'Krishna, remember to be careful. There will be a lot of people and food there. Don't get your clothes dirty.'

Krishna promised to be careful. Soon Ajji disappeared into the kitchen which was lined with people chopping and stirring and cooking. Outside, guests were pouring in and Vishnu Kaka was making sure everyone was served breakfast. Ajja was seen hurrying about with a bottle of phenyl in his hand. Rehmat Chacha was taking care of the flower decorations while Peerambhi Chachi was stringing piles of garlands. Children were playing all over the place, film songs played on the mike and there was a happy chaos everywhere.

After the wedding, during lunch time, while eating sweet pancakes of chiroti with badam milk, someone jostled Krishna and a big puddle of milk fell on her dress. She was grief-striken. Ajji consoled her. 'Don't cry. Silk can be washed and made to look just like new. That is the wonderful thing about it.' Seeing her tear-stained face she said, 'Today when we go home

I will tell you the story of how silk was made for the first time.' That made Krishna happy. That night, though Ajji was tired, she still told the children the story of silk.

— ✦ —

Did you know that silk was discovered in China?

A long time ago, in a tiny village in China, there lived a poor girl from a weaver's family. One day, the emperor was passing through the village and saw her working in the fields. He noticed her red cheeks and rosebud-like mouth, her proud bearing and her rough, work-worn hands, which meant she worked very hard through the year. He immediately fell in love with her and though he was much older, decided to marry her.

The girl married the ruler of the land and went to live in his palace as his beloved queen. But she was unhappy. She had grown up in the wide open spaces of the countryside, and now she was confined to a palace, magnificent though it was. She was used to working from dawn to night without a moment's rest, but now she had many servants to take care of her needs and did not know how to fill her time. In the village she had been surrounded by family and friends who exchanged news and gossip as they worked, but in the palace it was quiet and no one spoke out of turn. The emperor noticed his new wife was sad and tried his best to make her happy. He bought her grand clothes, jewels and artefacts, threw elaborate parties, hired the best musicians of the land to amuse her. Yet she was sad.

One afternoon, the empress sat under a mulberry bush in her garden, lost in her thoughts about her village. She slowly sipped hot water from a cup. Staring up at the blue sky, the girl remembered the birds that flew over her village. Then, sighing softly to herself, she picked up her cup to take another sip. But what was this! A cocoon from the mulberry bush had dropped into the hot water! Her first thought was to throw away the water and the cocoon. But then she took a closer look, and she saw some threads peeping out from the cocoon. Where had they come from? She pulled the threads. They were thin, strong and shiny. She kept pulling and a long line of thread came out. Now the empress had a great idea. She would take the thread from many cocoons and weave soft, strong cloth from it!

She called her servants and everyone got to work. They took cocoons out of the mulberry tree, dropped them in hot water, and removed the thread. They gathered a fair amount of yarn. Then the queen ordered a special weaving machine and wove the first piece of cloth using this new thread. Thus silk, the best and brightest form of cloth, was weaved.

The manufacture of silk spread throughout China. It was the cloth that only royalty could wear, and

was much in demand in lands as far away as Rome. The route through which silk was traded between China and Europe through Asia was called the Silk Route.

Now that the Chinese had learnt how to make silk cloth, they did not want to share this knowledge with anyone in the world. Generations of Chinese royalty were sworn never to reveal the secret to anyone. When princesses got married and went away to far-off lands, they were not allowed to tell anyone in their new home how silk was made.

Many, many years later, when a clever princess was leaving her house on getting married, as was the custom, her bags were searched carefully to check that she did not carry anything that would help her make silk. This princess had been weaving silk from a young age and wanted to continue to do so wherever she went. She had hidden the cocoons in her long, elaborate hairdo. No one thought of looking there! When she went to her husband's house, she took out these cocoons from her hair and started gathering silk thread! In this way, legend goes, the knowledge of how to make silk left China.

When Yama Called

One day, Ajji was sitting and stitching a tear in an old sari. The children came and sat around her. The holidays were finishing and they did not want to be away from her for even a minute. Meenu and Krishna affectionately put their arms around Ajji's neck and said, 'Ajji, why do you have so many wrinkles on your hand?'

'Because I am old,' said Ajji.

'Why do old people have wrinkles?' asked Meenu.

Ajji took off her glasses, which she wore only when sewing or reading, and said, 'Once upon a time I was also young like you. My skin was smooth and shiny. My hair was long and black. I had very sharp eyes and an excellent memory. But as I grew older, everything changed slowly.'

'We will all grow old like this one day, shan't we?' asked Divya.

'Yes, every living being gets old. It is a part of life. Come, I will tell you a story about old age.'

—

Many many years ago, there lived, in a little town, a man named Arun. He was a merchant and though not very rich, he lived comfortably enough. He had a large family of brothers, sisters, wife and children. He looked after them well, and in whatever way he could he also helped out the poor people in the town. He built rest houses for travellers, and in these there were dining halls where anyone could come and have a good, wholesome meal for very little money.

One day, while returning home from work, he happened to pass by one such rest house. It had a veranda where people stopped and rested. Sitting there, looking tired and hungry, was a stranger. He was a tall man. His clothes were travel-stained and showed that he had come from afar. With him was his horse, looking as tired and hungry as its master.

Seeing them, Arun's kind heart melted, and he went up to speak to the man.

'Where have you come from, my brother?' he asked. 'Why don't you step inside for a hot meal and some rest?'

The man looked up, gave a smile and said, 'The rest house is very popular. There is no room for me, and the dining hall is full too. I will wait here for a while, then be on my way. I'm sure I will find another place to serve me some food down the road.'

Arun would not hear of this. The thought that someone was going away without food and rest was too much for him. He insisted on the man coming back to his house with him. There he invited the traveller to share a meal with his family. The man was served lovingly and ate his fill.

While he sat eating, the man noticed that Arun was sometimes a bit absent-minded. It was as if something was on his mind, and he was worried. Once they had finished eating and had washed up, the traveller rose to leave. He thanked Arun for his kindness, then said, 'If you don't mind me asking, sir, I could not help but notice that you were a bit worried. I know I am a stranger to you, but perhaps it would help lighten your burden if you shared your worries with me.'

But Arun only smiled and shook his head. He did not want to share his thoughts with the stranger.

Then the man said, 'Perhaps if I show you who I really am you will confide in me.'

And in a trice the man changed. He was no longer a tired traveller, but a god, resplendent in shimmering clothes with a crown on his head. His horse changed into a buffalo, and the man introduced himself, 'I am Yama, the lord of death. Now will you tell me what's wrong?'

Seeing this Arun nearly fainted. The lord of death had just shared a meal with him! 'Wh-what are you doing on earth, my lord?' he gasped.

Yama smiled and said, 'Oh, I like coming here once in a while, and seeing what everyone is doing. So, what's bothering you?'

Arun replied, 'You see, I need to grow my business more, but today I was not feeling very well. If anything happened to me, who would look after my large family?'

Yama nodded seriously. 'Don't worry, child,' he comforted. 'I have seen what a hardworking, kind-hearted person you are. You invited me home and let me have a meal with you, knowing me only to be a tired and weary traveller. I will do one thing. When it is time for you to leave the earth and come with me, like all living things have to do one day, I will not come all of a sudden. I will let you know many days in advance, so you can prepare yourself and your affairs for the time you have to go away with me.'

Arun bowed to the lord in gratitude when he heard this and Yama vanished.

Years went by. Arun became an old man. His business had grown many times over, his children and brothers and sisters were all well looked after. He had few worries left.

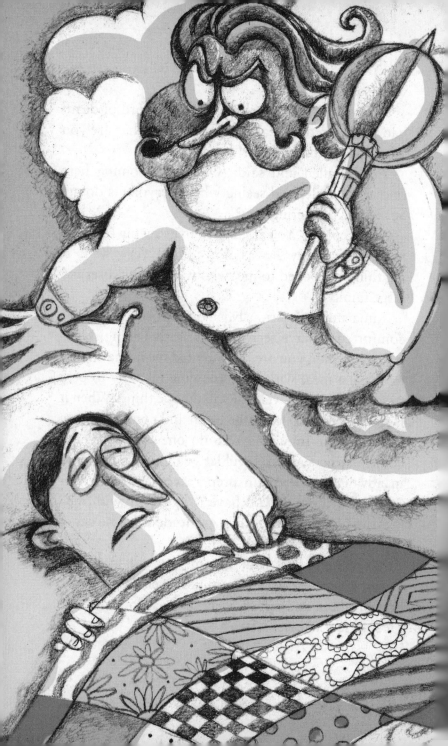

One night, he went to bed and had a dream. He saw Yama standing in front of him. Yama was holding out a hand towards him and saying, 'Come, it is time for you to go away with me.'

Arun was terrified. 'But lord, you had promised you would tell me days in advance before I would die. How can I come away right now?'

A small smile appeared on Yama's lips. 'But child, I did give you a warning. I made your hair turn white, I made your back stoop with age, I made your teeth fall out one by one. These were all indications that your time on earth is coming to an end.'

'But these things happen to every man and woman! How could these be a warning only for me!'

Yama nodded, 'Yes, they do happen to everyone. And when they do, men and women should start getting ready to meet me. Life has to come to an end, there is no escape.'

Arun now understood. He looked back on his days and realized that even without meaning to, he had been preparing for this. His children looked after his business, all his work was done. There was nothing stopping him from going away with his old friend Yama.

He climbed on the buffalo behind Yama. 'Let's go,' he said. And off Yama went away with him.

The Unending Story

Today Ajja, Ajji and Vishnu Kaka were all feeling sad. The children's holidays were nearly over, and it was nearing the time when they would go back to their homes. For three weeks the houses had echoed with their laughter, games and quarrels. Now all would be quiet once again, till they returned for the next holiday. The children too were feeling sad, and had gathered around their grandparents in a tight little group. Raghu the eldest said, 'We had more fun this holiday then we've ever had. Even more than when we visited Disney Land. And it was all because of the stories.'

Ajja said, 'When I was still working as a schoolteacher, I always found it was so much easier to get my students' attention when I told the lessons in the form of stories.'

Anand said, 'I find it really boring to read history from a book. But if you tell us the stories from history I'm sure we will remember everything!'

Everyone now turned their bright eyes on Ajji. 'How can you tell us only one story even on this last day, Ajji! We want more!' they clamoured.

But Ajji shook her head. 'If you eat only pickles and laddoos will you be healthy? Stories are like that. You can't spend all your time listening to stories. Then it will be boring. Like the unending story that a king once had to hear.'

⁓

'I want a story! And that's an order!' shouted King Pratap Singh of Mayanagar. King Pratap was only fifteen years old, and still a boy at heart. He didn't like being a king much, because he was supposed to be doing serious things like keeping the law, listening to his people's problems and all kinds of dreary things like that. The only part he liked about being a ruler was everyone had to obey him! How he loved giving orders and making all kinds of demands. And what he loved the most was listening to stories! Every day, he insisted on listening to at least ten stories. All the storytellers in his kingdom lined up at his court. They told him funny stories, scary stories, magical stories and anything else that came to their mind. King Pratap listened to all with rapt attention.

He loved stories and storytellers so much that whenever he heard a good tale he would shower the teller with gold, silver and all kinds of wonderful presents. His ministers sighed and shook their heads and tried to explain, 'Your Majesty, stories are all very well, but you should be listening to them after your work is done! Your people need you to do so many things for them. If you spend all your time wrapped up in fantasies, how will the land prosper?'

But King Pratap paid no attention. It was stories he wanted, and stories he would get. But how long could the people provide him with stories? Soon the tales began to dry out. Some tried to cleverly tell him ones they had related long back, but Pratap was sharp as a needle. 'I've heard that one! Off with his head for repeating a story!'

Oh, how his ministers had to plead with him to pardon the culprits!

Finally, disgusted with all the storytellers in his land, the king announced, 'I want someone to tell me a story that will go on and on, till I ask him to stop. Anyone who can do this will get half my kingdom as a prize!'

His ministers were even more horrified at this. Half the kingdom to some woolly-headed writer and teller of stories! How horrible! They all tried to show the king the foolishness of his ways, but he was adamant. A story that lasted for days, even weeks, was what he wanted and that was that!

Soon a long line of men and women appeared at his court. Each one wanted to win the big prize. But none of their stories were good enough for King Pratap.

'Boring!' he shouted at some.

'Rubbish!' he yelled at others.

'Cock and bull!' he bellowed at yet others.

Meanwhile work on the kingdom's affairs had come to a stop. All the ministers were sitting wringing their hands and wondering how to bring back their king to solving all the important issues. Finally the chief minister, who was wise and clever, had an idea.

The next day, a scruffy, crazy-looking man turned up at the court. His hair was in a mess, his clothes were half torn and on his feet he wore torn shoes from which his toes stuck out. He marched up to the palace and demanded to be given an audience with the king. The guards sighed and let him in. They were used to having all kinds of characters turning up at the gates wanting to tell stories to the king.

The old man was admitted into the king's chamber. There he made himself comfortable, drank a huge jug of water, and without introducing himself, started his story:

'This story begins in a humble farmer's field. The farmer had toiled days and weeks and months

and grown a bumper crop of sugar cane. He sold the sugar cane to the nearby sugar factory and they made sacks and sacks of sugar out of it. Everyone was so happy. All this sugar would be sold in the markets and make everyone very rich! That year their children would get nice new clothes, their stores would be full of food and their wives would be very happy with them!

'Now all that sugar had to be stored and kept carefully till the sacks could be taken to the market to sell. The factory people poured the sugar into many sacks and lugged them into a storeroom. In the storeroom who would you find, but a colony of ants. They had decided that building their house near such a ready supply of their favourite food was a very good idea, and were always on the lookout for new batches of sugar to be stored there.

'No sooner had the sacks been kept than the lines of ants marched up to them. They found little holes to make their way in and the first ant went into the first bag of sugar, took one sugar crystal and went back.

'The next ant went into the bag and took a crystal and returned home.

'Another went into the bag and took a crystal and returned home.

'Yet another went into the bag and took a crystal and returned home . . .'

So on and on the storyteller droned. King Pratap found he had nearly dozed off, the day had passed by and he was still listening to the same story.

'Stop! Stop!' he ordered. 'I will listen to the rest of the story tomorrow.'

The next morning the old man turned up as usual and started from where he had left off the previous day. 'Yesterday I was telling you how the ants came and picked up the sugar crystals. Now the next ant went towards the bag of sugar and took a crystal and went back home. Another went and took a sugar crystal and returned home. Another ant . . .'

The story went on and on like this. Lunch and dinner passed by but nothing new happened. By now King Pratap was bursting with rage. How dare anyone tell him such a boring story? 'What kind of a story is this?' he complained. 'What will happen next? What happened to the farmer?'

But the old man only smiled and said, 'Have patience, Your Majesty. That year the yield was very good and there were thousands of bags of sugar. I have to tell you how the ants collected all the sugar.'

'Oh stop! Stop!' Pratap shouted. 'Stop this boring story at once!'

The man now stood up and said, 'Fine, if you are ordering me to stop, I have won the prize. Give me half your kingdom!'

The king was in a dilemma now. He had announced a competition and prize no doubt, but could he honestly give away half the kingdom to this crazy-looking storyteller with his boring tales?

As he sat pondering, the man grinned even wider, and took off his dirty robe, rubbed off the dirt from his face and shook back his shaggy white hair. Everyone was astonished. Why, this was the chief minister himself!

'Don't worry, Your Majesty,' the minister told his overjoyed king. 'I did not want half your kingdom. I only wanted to show you how you were wrong to neglect your work and listen to stories night and day. Your people deserve a good king, someone who will work hard to look after them; someone who will think of his own happiness only once his people are happy. That's what good kings do, you know. Not just giving orders and enjoying yourself.'

Poor Pratap looked ashamed at this. Yes, he had been an extremely selfish king. From now on, story time was only at night, after all his work was done.

—

So that was how the summer holidays ended. Everyone packed their bags and reached the station. Their mothers had come to take them back home. Ajja, Ajji, Vishnu Kaka, Damu, Rehmat Chacha—everyone had come to see them off. No one felt like leaving Ajji's side and Meenu kept hugging her till she had to board the train.

Soon the train puffed out of the station. The children leaned out to wave their goodbyes. Slowly Shiggaon got left behind. But the children would continue to remember their Ajja and Ajji and everyone else, and all the stories, which would remain with them forever. And they would be back, during the next summer holidays, when they would hear so many more . . .